I0679280

CABO DARKNESS

CABO
BOOK 5

ROBERT WISEHART

ROUGH
EDGES
PRESS

Cabo Darkness
Paperback Edition
Copyright © 2025 Robert Wisehart

Rough Edges Press
An Imprint of Wolfpack Publishing
1707 E. Diana Street
Tampa, FL 33610

roughedgespress.com

All rights reserved. No part of this book may be reproduced in any form
or by any electronic or mechanical means, including information
storage and retrieval systems, without express written permission from
the publisher, except for the use of brief quotations in reviews. Any use
of this publication to train generative artificial intelligence (AI)
technologies is expressly prohibited.

This book is a work of fiction. References to historical events, real
people, or real places are used fictitiously. Any similarity to real
persons, living or dead, is purely coincidental and not intended by the
author.

All brand names and product names used in this book are trademarks,
registered trademarks, or trade names of their respective holders.
Wolfpack Publishing is not associated with any product or vendor in
this book.

Paperback ISBN 978-1-68549-467-4
Ebook ISBN 978-1-68549-466-7
LCCN 2025946331

CABO DARKNESS

PROLOGUE

EVEN BEFORE HE FIRED, he knew the shot was good.

It happened that way sometimes. There was no feeling like it.

Athletes called it being in the zone, that rare moment when training, mind, body, and purpose come together with effortless fluidity.

After watching for seven days, he knew the target's routine down to the last twitch. The tall, tanned, gray-haired man was exactly on time, bursting with self-importance as he strode from the big house to the waiting helicopter fifty yards away. As usual, three young lackeys trailed behind the target like puppies following a mastiff as he barked last-minute orders.

Lying with his legs spread to absorb the recoil, he was so concentrated that he did not feel the hard New Mexico desert beneath him as he readied his weapon, a bolt-action Sako TR6 M10. The shot was on the outer limits of the Sako's range, but there was no wind, the scope gave him the necessary optics, and the bipod supporting the barrel was rock steady. The sand-colored Sako never let him down.

It happened just as he knew it would. Before stepping

up into the helicopter, the gray-haired man turned to the right to take his briefcase from one of the lackeys, in effect facing the assassin three-quarters of a mile away. He fired, and the target's head exploded in a shower of bone, blood, and brain matter, shattered by a .338 caliber projectile moving at almost twice the speed of sound.

With calm and precise movements, he removed the bipod, folded it, and fitted it and the Sako into the sling across his chest. He slid backward five yards, then pivoted one hundred and eighty degrees so that he could crawl forward. After another ten yards, he eased into an arroyo that allowed him to stand without risk of being seen and jog toward the all-terrain vehicle that was so well concealed by a camouflage tarp that it took him a moment to spot it.

Even though he was always careful to properly hydrate in the desert, he suddenly felt dizzy and light-headed. Instead of pulling off the tarp and stowing it away, he fell to his knees like a deflating balloon before tumbling over on his side. There was no strength in his arms and legs, and a sudden, terrible pain in his gut made him double over like a jackknife.

Before he passed out, he marveled that a life devoted to discipline and control would end with neither one.

CHAPTER 1

I WAS DRINKING my second cup of coffee and catching up on *The New York Times* news on my iPad when the smooth notes of Dave Brubeck's *Take Five* signaled that I had a call.

A glance told me who it was—Valencia, the Cabo San Lucas chief of police.

As usual, he did not waste time. "I need to see you right away. Are you at home?"

"I am. What's going on?"

"Twenty minutes?" he asked, ignoring my question.

"I'll be here," I said. "You haven't been to the new place yet. Know how to get here?"

"I do," he said.

After my wife died, for too long I rattled around in our big house on the beach just outside of Cabo San Lucas before deciding that it was too big for one person and at the same time crowded with too many memories. I sold the place for more than three times what we paid and spent part of the profit on a condo in the hills above town. Unlike at the beach house, I couldn't see the famous Los Cabos arch from my new home, but the city and ocean view were still spectacular. The condo was just the right size for me, and for a monthly fee, somebody else did all the work.

Whatever Valencia wanted, I knew that he'd want coffee. If I drank as much in a week as he did in a day, I'd be clawing at the ceiling. Brewing a new pot, I puzzled over his tone, which was uncharacteristically abrupt. Unless you crossed him, never a wise move, Valencia was a man of polish, style, and manners.

The coffee stopped burbling just as the doorbell rang. That was one disadvantage of the new place. We had a guard at the gate, but I missed the crunch of tires on gravel that gave warning of visitors.

I opened the door and was so surprised that I staggered back like someone had punched me in the chest.

CHAPTER 2

V ALENCIA WAS NOT ALONE.

To his left was Big Eddie Heenan, all six feet, six inches and two-hundred-forty-five pounds of Southern Californian. He was dressed as usual in a pair of slim-cut jeans, a pullover shirt with gathered sleeves straining at his upper arms, and bright red hand-tooled cowboy boots that probably cost three or four times as much as my fifty-eight-inch TV.

On Valencia's right was Chango Suarez, the best cop that I, or anybody else, ever knew. As usual, Chango's outfit would make fashionistas weep. His only concession to the Cabo climate was a white short-sleeved *guayabera* shirt that his wife probably bought for him, along with pleated slacks that might have been dynamite in, say, 1961, and wing tips. Nothing says Cabo San Lucas like brown wing tips.

Finally retired from the San Francisco Police Department, Chango worked independently as a consultant to law enforcement agencies across the country. I wasn't sure exactly what that meant, except that he made a lot more money for a lot less work. Hardly anybody ever shot at him, too.

Valencia broke my stunned silence. "May we come in?"

After manly hugs and pounding on backs, I ushered the trio into my tile-chrome-and-white-leather living room and took coffee orders—yes for Valencia and Chango, no for Heenan.

Back in the kitchen, I tried to get my head around the strange mood that entered with my visitors. The three toughest men I knew seemed...what? Nervous? Apprehensive? That was close, I thought, as if they were taking on something they dreaded.

But what did that have to do with me?

I returned with the coffee, along with another cup for myself, and settled into my big leather chair.

"Okay, what's going on?" I asked. "It's not like you guys accidentally ran into each other in the line to get into Cabo Wabo."

Heenan looked at Valencia and Valencia looked at Chango.

"Maybe you should go ahead, Chango," suggested Heenan. "It started with you."

Chango gathered himself with a sip of coffee and a deep breath. "I know a guy with the Feebs."

Feebs was Chango's word for anybody with the federal government, from the FBI to the post office.

"He's got a big mouth and tries too hard to seem like a real insider, but once in a while, he actually knows something. He told me how the Feebs accidentally got their hands on a guy who just may be the world's most successful assassin."

"Accidentally?" I asked.

"Entirely. You remember a pig named Goldstein, the billionaire pal of other billionaires who ran what amounted to a sex slave operation on the side? Some of the girls were as young as twelve years old, and he always kept a few around to entertain himself and his pals. Over the years, a lot of people suspected something bad was going on, but they all looked the other way. He was too connected."

"But didn't they finally get him?" I asked.

"Yeah, they did. Sort of. Except that with his money and lawyers, he'd die of old age before seeing the inside of a jail."

Chango drained the last of his coffee and declined a refill.

"It turns out that Goldstein got his head blown off a couple of weeks ago. So far, the Feebs have managed to keep a lid on it."

Heenan couldn't keep silent any longer. "It was a righteous shot, too," he said. "More than three-quarters of a mile."

Chango didn't appreciate the interruption and gave Heenan a look that could have stunned a water buffalo. Fortunately, Heenan was stronger than any water buffalo.

"Among his homes around the world, Goldstein had a place in New Mexico, something like fifty thousand acres near the border, not far from Las Cruces. He was walking from the house to a waiting helicopter when he was shot."

"I assume that's the work of the killer you mentioned," I said.

Chango changed his mind and decided that he did want more coffee. He kept talking while I got it.

"Yeah, it was. He had an all-terrain vehicle ready, one of those three-wheel jobs, and would have gotten away except he collapsed before he could even get the camo off.

"With their fearless leader down and his brains splattered all over southern New Mexico, Goldstein's stooges scattered like scared rabbits. Finding the guy who shot their lord and master was the furthest thing from their minds. They were too busy saving their pale white asses after grabbing everything of value they could get their hands on, starting with cash and jewelry. They even pulled several million dollars' worth of art off the walls. The Feebs have already run down most of 'em, and they'll get the rest eventually.

"Nobody will say this out loud, but Goldstein's death did everybody a favor, so the Feebs didn't exactly break their backs looking for the killer. They did a quick air search, but between the camo on the vehicle and the camo the killer was wearing, they didn't see anything. Assuming whoever it was had long gone, they saw the nothing they expected to see.

"It wasn't until a couple of days later that a routine border patrol looking for illegals found the killer, baked to a crisp and dehydrated as hell. He's recovered from that, mostly, but it turns out he has pancreatic cancer and didn't know it. That's why he collapsed. Until late in the game, a lot of the time, there aren't any symptoms to speak of, at least nothing you'd recognize as symptoms if you didn't know you had cancer, and it moves fast. Basically, it's a death sentence. Just a matter of when.

"It wasn't until he started talking that the Feebs realized what they had. This guy has been *the* primo assassin for more than thirty years. He worked all over the world. Personal or political, it didn't matter. He's killed everybody from heads of state to grandma's next-door neighbor whose dog barked too loud. He knows all the ways there are to kill in any circumstance. He could be so subtle that nobody suspected it wasn't an accident or a natural death, or brutal and messy when somebody wanted to send a message. Nobody seemed out of his reach. It's been a long time since he worked for anything less than a million a kill, and that's his low end."

"At least it cuts down on client riff-raff," I said. "Chango, I wasn't sure guys like that really existed. I thought they mostly were a creation of movies and novels. I've never run into one, at least not that I know of."

Chango nodded again.

"It's like you said, *mostly* these globe-trotting super assassins *are* fiction. There probably aren't more than two or three in the world, and this guy was head and shoulders above anybody else."

"If I may add something," asked Valencia, receiving a nod from Chango.

"There long were rumors of such a person, but no one ever got a glimpse, much less found any kind of trail to follow. I remember from my time with Interpol in Europe, we weren't even sure he was real. Maybe it was several killers that stories and gossip conflated into one? Or was it more myth than reality, a legend born from a thousand rumors? Nobody knew anything. He was that good."

"You remember Whitey Bulger?" Chango asked.

"Sure, he was the Boston mobster who finally got caught someplace in California after being on the run for so long he'd become an old man," I said. "If I remember it right, he was beaten to death in prison."

Talking about it brought more details to the surface.

"His, ah, peers weren't pleased when they found out he was a federal informant who got protection from prosecution at the same time he ran a big chunk of the Boston mob," I said. "Something like that anyway."

"He was on the receiving end of the old lock-in-a-sock beatdown," Heenan said. "Apparently, this guy did it."

"Everything he says checks out," Chango said, taking

back control of the conversation. "He won't talk about some things, though he won't say why. But he's already solved more cold cases than Dick Tracy. He said something about the dead having their say, whatever that's supposed to mean. Maybe it's because this time he's the one who's dying. That does have a way of concentrating the mind. But nobody really knows."

Chango's Dick Tracy reference drew a puzzled look from Valencia, who apparently was not up on ancient American comic strip history. Hard to believe.

"How the hell did he pull the Bulger thing off? And I thought they had the guy who did it, or at least helped get it done."

"That's the beauty of it," Chango said. "Apparently, one of the things this guy does best is misdirection. When you get 'em looking at somebody else, it means they're not looking at you. The character they arrested never knew what hit him.

"I don't have the details, but it's probably not that hard to break into prison. I mean, who the hell does that? Getting out's the problem. It looks like he money-whipped a couple of guards to get inside wearing a guard's uniform, beat Bulger to death, got out with their help, and then over time killed the guards in unrelated ways to leave behind no one who could talk. This guy's better than Houdini. The Feebs still don't even know his real name. The ID he had on him said Nathan Brittles, but he's probably got more false IDs than fingers."

"Not to mention a sense of humor," I said. "Nathan Brittles was the name of John Wayne's character in *She Wore a Yellow Ribbon*, one of his best."

I had a bad feeling about where this was going, but I let it play out. With luck, maybe I was wrong.

"So what does all this have to do with why you guys showed up here?"

For a moment, the three men gazed deeply at their footwear before Valencia answered.

"Ethan, it looks like this man killed your wife."

CHAPTER 3

THE NEXT THING I KNEW, I was shouting. I just didn't know what I was shouting or who I was shouting at.

From what seemed like far away, I heard Heenan say, "Hey! He mumbled something. I think he's coming around."

"I'll get him some water," Chango said.

"Valencia, what did you say this was?" Heenan asked.

"It is called dissociation. In some form, it's a way of protecting yourself from things you can't control. You go away inside your own head, even though it's involuntary. If it's a mild episode, there's a good chance nobody notices because you still function. You just seem a little vague, as if you're not paying attention or you're daydreaming. With dissociation episodes, the worst fear is that, in the most severe cases, you go away and never come back. I'm simplifying a complicated thing, of course. But that's the essence of it."

"Sounds like you know a lot about it," Heenan said.

"I knew that Ethan suffered from it, or used to, and I wanted to know more about it. He doesn't like to talk about it, but from what little he's told me, I think this is his first episode in a long time."

Chango put the glass to my lips, holding the back of my head in his other hand. I slurped until I had enough and feebly waved to make him stop before I drowned.

I didn't enjoy being talked about like I wasn't in the room. It was time to rejoin the world.

After two tries, I finally got my eyes open and felt like an overachiever. I took the ice-water glass from Chango and held it in both hands. I slowly moved it across my forehead and then held it against each eye. The cold glass helped bring me all the way back.

Valencia was right. This hadn't happened in so long that I'd forgotten how much I hated it, and how much it scared me.

"How long?" I asked, my voice a weak croak.

"Ten minutes, or so," Chango replied.

I pushed myself erect in the chair.

"I'm okay. Really."

I could see that no one believed me, but it was time to move on. As I regained control, my voice was already stronger.

"All right, talk to me. What makes you think that Dina was murdered and this guy did it?"

"The Feeb with the big mouth knows that I've spent some time down here, though he doesn't know about you or anything specific," Chango replied, resuming his old position on the couch.

"He said the killer mentioned a murder in Cabo that he made look like a diving accident, though he didn't say when or name any names. With so much else to look at, the Feebs didn't pursue it. They might get around to it later, but I doubt it."

A few months after we moved to Cabo San Lucas from Southern California, Dina took up diving the way she did everything, with massive enthusiasm. Once she got the hang of it, she went out almost every chance she got. I rarely went along because I liked that she had her own interest, something that was hers and not shared with me, except in the telling.

There was no reason to think that what happened was anything other than what it seemed to be—a tragic accident as a result of an equipment malfunction. It happens. I left it at that. She was dead and I didn't give a damn about anything else.

If he suspected anything, Valencia would have been on it like a rabid wolverine. But a hundred miles north in the Gulf of California was way out of his jurisdiction. There was no reason to pursue it anyway. We all assumed that it was what it seemed to be because there was no reason to think it was anything else.

"The bottom line is that the killer is willing to talk to you," Chango said. "I know the guy who runs the New Mexico State pen outside of Santa Fe, which is where they're keeping him. He'll give you time with him, but it's got to be soon, fast, and secret. The killer doesn't have long to live, and it can never get out that he *did* talk to you, even after he dies. The Feebs and their many power-hungry agencies aren't even talking to each other about this. And they're sure not telling the other countries where this guy made kills, even high-level political kills, though they might use the information as a bargaining chip down the road if they find out who wanted it done. I have no doubt that our own government used him, too, probably another reason why they're keeping everything tight."

"That doesn't surprise me," I said. "Instead of *E Pluribus Unum,* the US motto should be Secrets R Us."

"Ethan, you should know that we debated telling you at all," Heenan said. "I mean, what good would it do? But we figured it's not our place to decide. If you want to talk to him, and what you do with the information you get should be your call, not ours."

I didn't have to think about it, though I probably should have.

"Hell, yes, I want to talk to this character," I said. "Exactly how do I go about it?"

CHAPTER 4

"WE KINDA THOUGHT that's how you'd want it." Heenan glanced at the others, who nodded in return. "I took the liberty of setting it up, assuming the timing works for you."

Heenan explained that he arranged for me and Chango to fly to Albuquerque the next morning. We'd pick up a rental car at the Albuquerque airport and drive an hour or so north to Santa Fe, spend the night, then drive to the state penitentiary outside of town early the next morning.

"I'm told it's better to get to this guy early in the day," Chango explained. "In his condition, he runs out of gas by afternoon."

"Like I said, everything's taken care of, assuming you approve," Heenan said. "I got the flights, the car, and the hotel. You'll stay at the La Fonda, a nice place just off the Santa Fe plaza, for as long as you need. It's all easy to cancel if you change your mind."

That was classic Heenan. Anyone who figured him for a muscle head was badly mistaken. He was smart enough to use being underestimated to his advantage.

He was, among other things, brilliant with money. It

came so easy that it wasn't a challenge anymore. He kept his skip tracing business because he liked the action, but he certainly didn't need it. His growing fortune was a tool that he used for his personal pleasure and to help friends when they needed it.

I was pretty well off, too, and he knew it. But I also knew better than to argue.

Anticipating my next thought, Heenan explained, "Chango's gotta go with you because he's your way in. You know how it is. Chango knows almost everybody. Valencia has his day job. And I have a, ah, troublesome history in that part of the world. If certain people there found out I was with you, it would do you no favors."

"Sounds good to me," I said, pushing against the arms of the chair as I rose to my feet. "But if we're leaving tomorrow morning, I have a few things to take care of. You guys are welcome to stay here tonight, and Heenan can stay here while Chango and I are gone."

"Thanks, but Valencia has us comped at the Pueblo Bonito Rose over on Medano Beach," Heenan said. "Our stuff is already there. That's where we stayed last night."

"I will drive you to the airport in the morning," Valencia added. "Smooth the way so there's not so much standing in line. I will pick you up when you return, too."

"Okay, but like I said, there are some things I have to do before leaving the country, even if it's only for a few days," I said. "Some of it's business and some of it's personal. Feel free to hang around here, but I've got to get moving."

After setting a time for Valencia to pick us up in the morning, we agreed to meet again to go over what we found out when Chango and I returned from New Mexico.

I didn't say thank you. I didn't need to. They knew.

CHAPTER 5

THERE WAS A LOT GOING ON, and I wanted to see my shrink before leaving in the morning. The dissociation episode made me feel like a recovering alcoholic who hadn't had a drink in years and suddenly goes on a bender.

When the psychiatrist I worked with retired, he referred me to Alfred Tasker, a colleague who was now a happy expat in Cabo San Lucas. Between endless rounds of golf and a fair amount of traveling, he still worked with a few patients just to keep his hand in, along with keeping the tax advantages that come with working for yourself. I'd been seeing him for a while, but we weren't on a regular schedule. It was more of an as-needed basis, and today I needed it.

I called and explained the situation. He said he could see me right away. Tee time wasn't until mid-afternoon.

Tasker lived up in Pedregal, the oldest of the ritzy sections in Cabo San Lucas, a once sleepy little fishing town that was now full of ritz. With its dazzling marina and ocean views and close proximity to town, Pedregal was one of the first areas to go upscale once the southern tip of the Baja peninsula was discovered by the Hollywood celebrity world back in the early 1950s, mostly for its fantastic sport fishing, although these days there might be more golf than fishing.

At one time, there were so many second homes of the rich and famous in Pedregal that it was known as Cabo's version of the Hollywood Hills. Eventually, most of the swells went on to frolic in new playgrounds and more anonymous money, along with a few more swells, moved in.

I briefly considered Pedregal myself, but decided that it was overpriced. It wasn't new enough for my taste either. I didn't want to spend a lot of time and money remodeling, and the main road winding up and down the hillside did not make me tremble with pleasure.

I rang the bell, Tasker met me at the door and led the way to his comfortable office. One of the things I liked about him was that he looked like a psychiatrist, which seems silly, but I found it comforting. He was slightly overweight, with a beard more salt than pepper, and always had a pipe in his hand, though I never saw him light up. On this day, it was an expensive-looking briar with an elegant curve to the stem.

"I've always wanted to ask you something," I said, settling into what I thought of as the patient's chair. "Are the pipes just props or do you actually smoke?"

"Two or three bowls a day," he said. "But only outside. My wife won't allow it indoors. I do tend to fiddle with one from my rather large collection when I see patients. They seem to like it. Makes me seem avuncular and trustworthy, I suppose."

I told him what happened, with as much detail as I could remember. As usual, he let me talk without interruption.

When I finished, he asked, "How do you feel?" I knew

that was coming. Along with "What's going on?" it was almost always Tasker's opening question.

"I'm okay, really," I said. "I can't make it any clearer than that."

"You seem a little defensive," he said.

"That's because I feel like nobody believes me. Despite what everybody, including me, keeps calling the episode, like it's part of a TV series, or something, I feel removed from it all. Not in a spaced-out way, but as if this is just another case. It's been long enough since Dina died that I have some distance. I know that's probably a defense mechanism, or whatever you shrinks might call it, but it works for me."

Tasker thought for a moment, stuck his unlit pipe in his mouth, and nodded his approval.

"It works for me, too, generally, though I do think you'll probably have to deal with this in a more direct emotional way sometime down the road, after the crisis, or case, is over.

"By the way, I'm not particularly worried about your brief dissociation, brief being the important word. You were blindsided by an astonishing revelation. It would have shaken anyone, especially anyone with your history. You seem to have dealt with it for now."

"That's good to hear. I—"

Tasker held up one hand, palm out like he was signaling for an oncoming car to stop.

"But with all that said, do you really think that pursuing this is a good idea?"

My explanation was long, but, as often happened, talking to the shrink helped coalesce my thinking.

Dina had no enemies, of that I was sure. Whoever killed her, or paid to have her killed, did it to get to me. It was a person of means, or they couldn't have paid for the best assassin in the world. They were patient, too, even if patience might have been forced on them by circumstances. Finding the assassin, the feeling out process, coming to financial terms, and then waiting while he scouted, planned the operation, and finally put the plan into action took time. Whoever it was could have contracted to have me killed, but they obviously wanted me to suffer and decided that murdering Dina was the best way to make that happen.

But suffer for what?

Sometime in my past, I must have done something that demanded the worst kind of long-term revenge, at least somebody thought so. Given the business I was in, I had to assume the link was professional rather than personal, which made it something to do with a past case.

But revenge is rarely as satisfying as anyone who craves it thinks it is. What if one day this person discovered that killing my wife wasn't enough and decided to come at me after all?

Maybe I was wrong. It wouldn't be the first time. But at least it gave me a place to start.

"So I don't think I have any choice but to pursue it. It's a matter of self-preservation," I concluded. "And I'm positive I'm not fooling myself when I say that."

As I talked, the shrink never stopped fiddling with his briar. Now that I knew he actually smoked, I could tell that he wanted to light up. The ceremony of packing the bowl with a favorite tobacco until it was just right, then stoking it up and puffing away probably helped coalesce *his* thoughts, too. But he feared the wrath of his wife.

"Sounds reasonable," he said with another approving nod. "I'm surprised your friends didn't think of that."

"I'm sure they did. But they didn't want to influence me one way or the other by bringing it up. They knew I'd come to it eventually and deal with it in my own way."

"They know you well," he said.

"And I know them."

"So everything depends on your talk with the killer," he said. "The information you gather dictates your next step."

"If there is a next step," I said. "I promise that if I see no path forward, I won't force it."

The session was over. Tasker rose to his feet, the briar clutched in one hand.

"If you want to talk anytime while you're gone or after you get back, please call," he said. "If I don't pick up, leave a message and I will get back to you within a few minutes."

"Even on the golf course."

"Especially on the golf course," he said, shaking his head. "You might even be doing me a favor. To put it in complex psychiatric terms, lately my short game sucks."

CHAPTER 6

NEXT STOP: The office.

Yes, I had an office. Employees, too, with insurance, benefits, vacations, and the all rest of it. Where did I go wrong?

It started with a high-profile case that involved a famously neurotic movie star, a ridiculously expensive and genuinely terrible movie shot in Cabo that went on to make gazillions of dollars worldwide, a kidnapping, a killer hurricane that almost did me, the movie, and the movie star in, and much other weirdness.

In Mexico, the United States, and parts of Europe, several newspapers and magazines, or news operations that were now mostly digital but still called themselves that, latched on to the story. I was prominently mentioned and my photo prominently displayed. The story spread to television news. For about twenty-four hours, I was hot stuff on CNN, Fox, and all the rest.

Suddenly, it seemed like all the world wanted to employ Ethan Cruickshank, celebrity detective and detective to celebrities.

When we moved to Cabo, I didn't want to get back into what I'd done in Southern California. One bad night on a kidnapping case there, I spiraled out of control and into serious dissociation. An innocent man was killed. Accidentally. By me.

Thanks to high-powered friends, good legal help, and the fact that I spent time in a mental hospital because I needed it, I weaseled out of responsibility but still took it hard. I probably took it even harder *because* I weaseled out of responsibility. One reason for our move to Cabo was to leave all that baggage behind.

But as someone very wise said, no matter where you go, you take yourself with you. In Cabo, it wasn't long before I was pulled into a case, and then another one, and one after that. Work led to more work, opportunities kept coming, and more often than not, I said yes.

When Dina died, I took on more cases so I wouldn't just sit around and brood. With the movie star business and the attention it brought, I decided that having a small agency might not be so bad. There might never be a better time to start. I told myself that if I didn't like it, I could always get out.

I set up an office in a building that was part of the big *Tesoro* complex on the Cabo San Lucas marina downtown. It was on the second floor to discourage drunken tourists from seeing the agency's sign, then stumbling up the stairs and through the office door so they could blubber for us to find their high school, or college, or some other long ago girlfriend-boyfriend who they only just now realized, after several margaritas, was their only true love.

Every PI on the planet is plagued by that kind of nonsense. Some happily take those cases because it's easy money for minimal work. I didn't want to be bothered. Now our office *was* the second floor, all of it, with fine views of expensive yachts from the big show windows.

Maria Arredondo, the office manager and receptionist, was fluent in Spanish, English, withering looks, and unspoken scorn. I owned the operation, but in her role as dragon in the doorway, she more or less ran the non-detecting part. She was experienced, somewhere in early middle age, and did not suffer fools gladly, which meant that I was a constant irritation. Beneath the hard shell, she was intensely loyal to both me and the agency.

I also hired two detectives. If business got any better, I'd soon need a third. I wasn't sure how I felt about getting bigger.

Mike Callahan was a veteran Chicago cop who was invalided out when he was shot during a drug bust. Though he fully recovered, Callahan knew opportunity when he saw it. A physical fitness fanatic who was an expert in several martial art disciplines, he took his fat pension and moved to Cabo San Lucas. While he didn't want to see snow ever again, Cabo was still close enough to easily get back to the US when he needed to. Mike handled most of the English-speaking clients.

Antonio Vargas came to us instead of joining the Cabo San Lucas Police Department because Valencia thought he'd be a better fit.

As the chief put it, "The young man could be something special, but I don't have time to work with him as much as he needs, especially with his authority issues."

Since I had a few authority issues myself, we got along fine. To my surprise, I enjoyed playing mentor, though I was careful to never let him know what I was doing. A half-Italian, half-Mexican Cabo native with all the energy and cockiness of youth, Tony was savvy beyond his years and after a short time, started handling most of the Spanish-speaking clients.

And then there was my digital nerd.

Until I met Ursula Silva, my image of a digital nerd was a pasty character with lank, unwashed hair and the muscle tone of a chocolate éclair who lived on a diet of junk food and energy drinks.

My digital nerd was a thirty-ish Brazilian with two master's degrees. From Ursula's perfect tan and dazzling white teeth to her midnight black hair and tawny legs, she made The Girl From Ipanema look like Gertrude Stein. I'd seen important and powerful men reduced to stammering fools in her presence. She was a consultant because she valued her independence too much to be anybody's employee. My agency was just one of her many clients. She did not hesitate to fire a client if she felt like it.

Ursula could do anything that was possible to do in the digital world, plus the occasional task thought to be impossible, and was confident enough to say when something could not be done. Her extensive and still growing knowledge of government and law enforcement data systems around the world, combined with magnificent disdain for restrictions on access, gave her just the right combination of temperament and expertise to suit my needs.

She did not come cheap. In addition to her hourly rate, I paid her a quarterly bonus to be available when we needed her and not just when she could work it into her busy schedule.

Every so often, she declared that we must have some expensive piece of technology and patiently explained what it did and its value to the agency, even though she knew I had no idea what she was talking about. I'd listen to her pitch, say yes, and she'd buy it. It was a pleasant, if sometimes expensive, ritual.

At the top of this unruly heap was me, though Maria might disagree. I cherry-picked the cases I personally took on. They usually fit into one of three categories: the unusual, the interesting, and the easy.

Other than that, I wasn't in the office much, though we did try to have weekly early morning meetings. I liked getting a bunch of smart people in the same room because that's where a lot of good ideas come from. So far, it was working.

I walked in the door and Maria greeted me with her usual blind adoration.

"Well, look what *el gato* dragged in," she said. "Do you need directions or something?"

"Flattery will get you nowhere, though it wouldn't hurt to try just once," I said. "Anybody else around?"

"Nope, just me, *el jefe's* humble *peon*."

"Tomorrow morning I'm going out of town—out of the country, actually—for a few days. I'm not sure exactly how long I'll be gone," I said. "I wanted to tell you guys and make sure I don't have anything coming up that I need to apologize for canceling."

"You're never here," she replied. "How could you have anything to cancel?"

"I take that as a no."

"Definitely," she said. "Is there anything else your faithful employees need to know, like perhaps which country you *will* be in and when you *might* be back?"

"For the time being, I choose to remain a man of mystery, though I will be reachable."

I wasn't just giving Maria a hard time, though that was always a pleasure. For now, the less anyone knew about where I was going and what I was doing, the better. I never got in trouble keeping my mouth shut.

As I headed out the door, Maria made her usual lunge for the last word.

"This has been a really informative conversation. I feel positively enlightened."

"It's good somebody is," I said.

CHAPTER 7

As PROMISED, Valencia drove us to the airport about forty-five minutes away on the other side of the peninsula, not far outside of San Jose del Cabo, a more quiet and traditional colonial town than raffish Cabo San Lucas.

I hoped for lights and sirens, but Valencia saved that for actual crime. He did escort us through the airport as promised, which allowed us to skip nicely over the pesky security lines. With only carry-on luggage, we had nothing to check.

The aircraft was, as usual, jammed full of tourists, many of them looking worn, scorched by the sun, and desperately hungover as they clutched their plastic bags with so-called bargains from the duty-free shops, along with other detritus collected during their romp in Mexico. Most of them looked like they needed a vacation instead of returning home from one.

Heenan booked us in business class. Knowing he wouldn't be disturbed by someone climbing over to get to their seat or climbing the other way to get to the bathroom, Chango was asleep about ten seconds after fastening his seat belt. I was determined to be not far behind, though I'd probably make it to take off. Sleep had not come easy overnight. Fortunately, I found it no problem to sleep on airplanes and intended to give this one my best shot.

Getting to Santa Fe from Cabo was no easy journey. After the drive to the Cabo airport, it was almost a three-hour flight to the Dallas-Fort Worth airport, followed by two hours on the ground, which included getting through immigration—we both had Global Entry, which made it a lot faster—and changing terminals on the tram. Then came ninety minutes in the air to the Albuquerque airport, where we snagged our rental car, which had all the personality of a potato on wheels, and motored up the interstate to Santa Fe.

With Chango driving, I let myself be boggled by the scenery, from the vibrant colors and unique light to the sheer rugged openness of it, at least until the jagged mountains in the distance. This was the west as it should be.

"Yeah, it's no wonder artists like it here," said Chango, who saw me gaping out the window as I hummed the theme from *The Magnificent Seven*.

"Been here before?" I asked.

Chango nodded. "My wife has relatives around Albuquerque and Bernalillo. I know the area pretty well. You?"

"A couple of times with Dina."

Chango did not pursue it, which I appreciated.

Leaving the interstate, we got to the La Fonda after a few twists and turns through downtown Santa Fe's narrow streets. The streets were lined with what looked like historic homes and buildings but probably weren't. A few were real adobe, though most pretended to be. Someone once described Santa Fe as an adobe Disneyland, which was just about right.

The La Fonda was just a few steps away from the

city's famous plaza, where the Native American vendors sell their handmade wares along the front of the old Governor's Palace. We parked the rental in the garage underneath the hotel and elevated to the lobby to check in.

Chango wanted to have dinner at The Shed, a renowned restaurant just a couple of blocks away, where the margaritas were as good as the traditional food, a rabbit's warren of dimly lit small rooms in a genuinely old building that seemed to go on forever. He had reservations for two, but I passed. I told him I was tired and would grab something in the La Fonda restaurant off the lobby.

I really wanted to be alone and get ready for what might be an ordeal tomorrow. Chango had no problem dining by himself, and we set up a time to meet for breakfast in the morning before driving to the state penitentiary fifteen miles south of town.

I didn't sleep well that night either. It was getting to be a habit.

CHAPTER 8

LIKE OTHER STATE penitentiaries I'd seen, the New Mexico version was set so far back from the main road that it wasn't visible.

Nobody wants to show off a prison, unless, like Alcatraz, it's a tourist destination and not a prison anymore. The blocks of buildings with the usual chain link fences, barbed wire, high walls, and security towers looked a little different and yet much the same as they did everywhere.

We parked outside the wall in the parking area and the warden met us at the guard gate. He introduced himself as Don Burnside. We took stock of each other as we shook hands. He looked to be in his early fifties, with graying hair starting to thin, though mostly concealed by expensive styling. The handshake was firm and the dark gray suit well cut so that it went a fair way toward hiding what was on the verge of a serious paunch. The white shirt was crisp. The initials DGB on one shirt cuff peeked out from the sleeve of his suit. I thought monograms were a silly affectation, but for some reason, my fashion tips weren't in great demand. The silk tie was dark blue with tiny white designs.

Burnside seemed permanently weary, as if the relentless grind of supervising some eight hundred hard-core criminals in what amounted to a giant, overcrowded pressure cooker was wearing him out from the inside. If his health didn't break first, a few more years on the job and he'd be a candidate for early retirement.

"I wanted to meet you here and escort you to my office, but you'll still have to go through security," he explained, guiding us inside to a counter where we handed over our cell phones, car keys, wallets, pens, and pencils. Everything except pocket lint.

One at a time, we passed through a metal detector and *then* we were wanded. Given that the history of the place included a couple of deadly riots, a little redundancy in the area of security wasn't a bad idea.

We followed Burnside upstairs and down the usual ugly institutional hall to his office, which could have belonged to the head of an academic department at a well-off college. Nice but not too expensive furniture, with a desk that was large but didn't resemble an aircraft carrier like some ego-strokers I'd seen.

A variety of books and other flotsam and jetsam filled the built-in shelves, including several photos of a smiling Burnside posing with various political hacks trying to look like they're just pleased as peaches to be there, along with a few trophies and plaques.

The only items on the desk were a Mont Blanc pen, an old-school cradle telephone that I assumed was for internal use, and a legal-size leather notebook opened to a blank yellow page with blue lines, as if waiting for someone to say something important enough to be written down with the Mont Blanc.

A big window on the wall to his left overlooked the yard, where a dozen inmates stood around doing nothing, unless you counted smoking. Burnside settled into a red leather chair behind the desk while we took the visitor's chairs on the other side.

"I'm sure Chango already told you the rules, but let me go over them again," he said. "You can't record anything. There can be no record that you were here. He doesn't have to talk to you. If he decides at the last second that he doesn't want to, then it's over before it starts. Chango trusts you, so I trust you, too. You can't tell anybody you were here. Doing this puts my career on the line, but I owe Chango."

"Everybody does," I said.

Seeing something in my face, Burnside nodded.

"I know about the two other guys. Chango says they're okay, so they're okay. But nobody else. Understand? Chango will wait here while you have your talk. I'll take you to him when you're ready. There's a telephone on the wall near his bed. When you're finished, pick it up and punch the number one. I'll answer and come get you."

"What about notes?" I asked. "I gave up my notebook and pen downstairs. I don't want to rely strictly on memory."

Burnside closed his leather notebook, turned it one hundred eighty degrees, and gently pushed it across the desk to me. He reached into the middle drawer of his desk and handed over a cheap plastic government-issue pen that just might last the day if I was careful. He kept the Mont Blanc.

"We took your pen and watch in case there was some kind of recording device hidden in them. You can't write down his name, or whatever name he gives you, my name, the name of this place, the day, the time, or even the words New Mexico," he said. "Nothing that can be traced back to here. To make sure, I'll look over your notes when you finish."

"Security cameras?" I asked. "They're all over the place. We'll probably show up every minute we're here. And our names must be somewhere."

For the first time, Burnside smiled.

"Wouldn't you know it? The cams are down, all of them. I have a feeling they'll be fixed by this afternoon, after you're gone. As for your names, you might have noticed that no one asked. Your names don't appear on any schedule of visitors. The guards don't know who you are. Once you leave, you were never here."

"How is he?" I asked.

Burnside shrugged. "He's doing okay for a dying man, I guess. I've talked to him a few times on my own and sat in on a couple of conversations with the federal guys just to get a sense of what's going on. He's not only one of the smartest men I've ever met, he knows just how smart he is.

"I doubt that you'll have much of a problem getting information, though he often seems to hold something back, for reasons no one knows. Maybe he's just playing with us? I have a feeling he would do that. Will the information you get be useful? I have no idea. You aren't official, so that may help him open up more than usual. But, like I said, I don't really know. He's a hard guy to read, and he obviously likes it that way."

"How long do I have?"

"A couple of hours, at least. Maybe the whole morning. He tires easily, but the feds won't be coming today. They don't want to wear him out, so they give him pretty frequent breaks. Though he says he doesn't want or need them, he clearly does and he knows it. He just doesn't want to admit it."

"What's he doing here at all? Why not a hospital or a federal facility someplace?

"Security, for one thing," Burnside replied. "Too many eyes at a hospital. Here, the parade of feds with their identical suits, shoes, haircuts, and self-importance doesn't call attention to itself.

"We turned part of our infirmary into a private room with all the necessary medical equipment. We have nurses on hand in eight-hour shifts, twenty-four seven. A specialist sees him every day, and someone is always on standby. We're just a few minutes to the nearest hospital in Santa Fe by helicopter. For the first time in my career, I can honestly say that anything we need, we get. No questions asked.

"As to why not a federal facility, his last kill, that guy Goldstein, was in New Mexico, and he was captured in New Mexico. The state's a little sensitive about being ignored, which happens all the time. Most people don't even know where it is and think you need a passport to get here. The governor would have pitched a loud and public hissy fit if the feds tried to move him someplace else, as if New Mexico wasn't competent or trustworthy enough to handle it. It turned out that the feds liked the relatively isolated location and agreed to let it stand."

"If the governor knows, then other people with the state must know, too," I said.

Burnside shrugged his answer. He couldn't do anything about that. "But they don't know about you," he said. "And I want to keep it that way."

"Does he know I'm coming and who I am?"

"Yes, to both. Surprise didn't seem like a good idea. After all, you want his cooperation. It's not like we can do anything to punish the guy. He promised not to rat me out to the feds about you coming in, and I believe him. I think he's honorable in his own way, which I know sounds kind of weird. He even seems eager to see you, which I don't understand either."

We looked at each other for a moment.

"You ready?"

I took a deep breath. "I better be."

CHAPTER 9

IT LOOKED LIKE A MOVIE SET, an excellent facsimile of a hospital room set against one wall and screened off from the rest of the infirmary on the other three sides, with a stack of equipment on a table next to the bed tracking the patient's vital signs.

Burnside didn't bother to introduce us, except to announce, "Your visitor is here."

He nodded at me, slipped behind a screen, and headed back out the door.

I didn't know what the assassin looked like before he was captured. Apparently there were no photos of him anywhere. The man in the bed seemed diminished, as if his ordeal in the New Mexico desert and now waiting to die in this spirit-deflating place had already drained much of the life out of him.

Except for his eyes.

They were a startling laser blue that radiated a sense of dominance that no doubt helped make him the master of his world for so long. When necessary, he probably used contact lenses to mask his eyes and the power in them because it was something anyone would remember, even if they only saw him for a few seconds.

He looked to be an inch or two under six feet, though it was hard to tell under the blankets. His hair was dark, and even with all the recent wear and tear, he looked younger than his suspected age.

"You are Ethan Cruickshank," he said, the voice soft and the words precise.

"And you're *not* Nathan Brittles."

He smiled at that. "Oh, but I have been, among others, off and on for many years."

"Don't tell me you have another ID that says you're Rooster Cogburn. That might be a bit much."

"*True Grit*." He smiled again. "No, one John Wayne character was quite enough. It amused me to keep it. All my other identities were random and frequently changed. Each one required something different from me."

He motioned across the room with a turn of his head.

"Please, pull up a chair."

I grabbed a metal folding chair propped against the wall, brought it to his bedside, opened it up, and sat down. He pressed a button that elevated the upper third of the hospital bed so we could see each other more easily.

"I'm told you know why I'm here," I said.

"Generally, but not specifically."

"You murdered my wife by somehow rigging her equipment while working for a dive company in Cabo San Lucas," I said. "I'm not interested in the details of how you did it, and I'm not looking for revenge. I don't even blame you for it."

He looked surprised at that, even if it was just a slight widening of his mesmerizing eyes. I was a little surprised myself. Despite what I said to Chango, Heenan, and Valencia, I wasn't really sure I felt that way until this moment.

"You were just the weapon," I explained. "That's all. From what little I know about you, your ego probably makes you believe you're more than that, perhaps even an artist of some kind, an artist in death who's always the smartest guy in the room."

I leaned forward in the chair with my elbows on my thighs to get closer and emphasize my point.

"The thing is, I don't care about any of your self-serving bullshit. I want to know everything you know about who hired you, how they went about it, how you communicated, what was said, and how you got paid. All the facts, thoughts, impressions, and conjectures that come to you. Even if some of the details don't seem important, I want to hear them anyway."

I risked coming on too strong. He might take offense and refuse to talk. But I thought it more likely that a man such as this would respect the direct approach. He was too smart and experienced to con or to be led where I wanted him to go. There was no reason and no time to play games.

"I thought you weren't interested in revenge," he said.

"I'm not. It wouldn't change anything, would it? But if whoever it is decides to come after me, I intend to be ready. I might even decide to be—"

"Proactive," he said.

"Yeah, something like that. They used to call it taking the initiative. What happens next depends a lot on what you tell me."

A nod. The room was so quiet I heard his hair rustle against the pillow.

"First, allow me to say that the people with the dive company are blameless, though I understand your wife's death cast a cloud over the company even before it went out of business thanks to the damage COVID did to tourism all over the world.

"It happened as you surmised. The company was always looking for instructors and underwater tour guides, especially if they spoke English. As it happens, I speak several languages. I also grew up on an island and have been diving since I was a boy. While the situation was perfect for my needs, I would have found a way no matter what. I always did.

"Getting hired was surprisingly easy. It helped that there's a sizable community of diving gypsies across the world, most of them afflicted by the Peter Pan syndrome."

"Meaning they never grow up," I said.

"Exactly. They are so in thrall to diving that it's like a drug," he said. "Most don't think of their future at all as they travel seasonally from one place to another. But what becomes of them if they're injured, get older, and find themselves pushed out by younger divers, or something happens and they can't dive anymore? Such practical thoughts rarely leave a mark on the blank slate of their minds."

"I presented myself as one of them, with all the appropriate mannerisms and necessary qualifications so that the company saw in me exactly what it expected—and wanted—to see. It helped that I look younger than I am, even now. I was hired on the spot with virtually no background check, although I was prepared for a rigorous one. As soon as I saw that your wife…"

"She has a name." I heard the bite in my own words, as if someone else said them. "Her name is Dina."

For some reason, getting this man to say her name was important to me. After a pause while we took each other's measure, he said, "You're right. I apologize. It was disrespectful.

"As soon as I saw that Dina was still on the learning curve as a diver, though no longer a beginner, I adopted the guise I needed to join the company. Afterward, I stayed on long enough to let what little investigation there was wobble to an end so as not to make anyone suspicious with a too-rapid departure.

"When the time came, I explained that I was leaving because the whole thing…how did I put it? I said that it gave me the creeps. Since business was already slowing down thanks to COVID, they were happy to be rid of me, and I easily disappeared.

"I know that was off the track you want to pursue," he said. "But I thought it might offer some perspective and absolve the company of guilt in case you had other ideas."

"Fair but unnecessary," I said. "Now tell me, who hired you?"

He took a while before answering.

"You will be disappointed to hear that I don't have a name. I often make it a point not to know a specific name or location, just as my clients don't know exactly who I am. There have been a few exceptions, all of them initiated by me, but most of the time, not knowing is safer for both of us."

I expected that answer while hoping for more. Digging into the identity and background of his *clients* increased the risk of his own exposure, and in his line of work, only a fool would reveal his own identity. Whatever he might be, this man was no fool.

"Why initiated by you?"

"There have been several government sanctions around the world, and I had to know exactly who employed me and why, so I could assess motive and risk. Simply asking wouldn't work because you will be shocked to hear that governments lie.

"The other reason is payment, or lack of it. I require half upfront and the rest when I carry out the assignment, plus expenses, which can run high, occasionally almost as much as the fee itself. Obviously there is no formal contract, and a handful of times, exceptionally stupid clients refused to make the second payment, mistakenly assuming that I couldn't do anything about it. I could not allow such behavior to pass, so I hunted them down and took the necessary measures."

It was easy to imagine what this man meant by *the necessary measures.*

"How were you paid to...?" I couldn't complete the question and swallowed it away. "How are you—were you—paid?"

He understood my meaning.

"I have been paid in every way, from deposits in a variety of constantly changing offshore accounts to precious gems and artwork. The latter I sometimes kept for myself for either my own pleasure or an anticipated rise in value. Twice, I was paid in real estate, which I immediately sold because they were locations that did not appeal to me.

"In this case, it was cryptocurrency, which was virtually untraceable at the time. While it still has its uses and appears to be making something of a comeback, government and law enforcement are slowly catching up, with emphasis on slowly. It's a sad fact that cryptocurrency users and investors became too greedy and brought too much attention to themselves.

"But such behavior is the nature of humanity, isn't it? Find a good thing and pillage it until it's worthless. For a time, cryptocurrency was the Wild West of the financial world, with few rules and virtually no oversight. It was perfect for my needs."

"How were you contacted?"

"Through what is popularly known as the Dark Net, or the Dark Web, which is not what most people think it is, like an exceptionally unsavory neighborhood in a big city, a place you might take a wrong turn and stumble onto it by accident. Most people don't even think it's real, or they've never even heard of it. But, as someone once said, the devil's greatest achievement was convincing the world that he didn't exist.

"The Dark Web is simply an area of the unindexed World Wide Web that can only be accessed by special anonymizing software, and even then, there are other hurdles to overcome, such as configuration and authorization. You don't get there, or get something there, by accident. For obvious reasons, the ugliness of child pornography is particularly popular, as are getting false IDs, drugs, weapons, and any number of illegal endeavors."

"Anonymizing?"

"Yes, I know," he said. "Dreadful, isn't it?"

This was not going well. I'd gone from not getting a name to not really knowing what he was talking about. I'd heard about the so-called Dark Web but knew nothing about it.

"You must have something more," I said. "Why else would you agree to talk to me?"

"I came away with some impressions, along with other bits and pieces that might add up to significance if interpreted correctly. I didn't like the man, though that was hardly pertinent. He was exceptionally crude and seemed to revel in it, like a caricature of an old-time mafioso, a dese, dems, and dos guy. Perhaps he'd seen too many old gangster movies and based his behavior on what he saw. That happens more often than you might think. Often people with little self-esteem behave the way they think they should behave because they have no sense of self.

"He seemed incapable of offering a sentence without

profanity, as if he spent so long behaving the way he thought a tough guy should behave, those adopted mannerisms became part of him. I believe him to be perhaps cunning in a low way, but not well educated or particularly bright.

"We communicated in several different ways because that is my preference. Regular habits breed complacency and one becomes predictable. We spoke only twice. He used voice distortion both times. Fortunately, I had a program that removes the distortion, offering a reasonable version of his real voice. I do that because it's easier to catch nuance, emphasis, and lies.

"Despite a serious smokers' cough that sometimes overwhelms him, he still smokes heavily. I know that because I heard the loud click of his lighter, a sound not often heard these days. The lighter is probably flashy and expensive. Gold, I would think. Someone like that always confuses gaudy with good taste.

"From his language, references, and voice, I would place him in late middle age, or perhaps early old age. Anger long ago replaced youthful vitality. Anger at what I have no idea. I am sure he is American. Judging by the timing of our communications, along with a few clues he accidentally dropped, it's likely that he lives in either the mountain or western time zones in the United States."

He licked his lips and swallowed with such effort it was almost painful to see.

"Would you mind pouring me a glass of water? The attending physicians say otherwise, but I don't think I ever recovered from the desert dehydration. I seem to always be thirsty. Talking this much makes it worse."

There were two glasses, a pitcher of water, and a bucket of ice on the bedside table. I used tongs to get ice into one glass, poured the water, and, at his request, held the glass to his lips while he drank.

He drained the glass and sighed.

"Thank you. When there's not much left to enjoy, simple pleasures are all that matter.

"Back to business," he said, pushing himself higher in the hospital bed. Just making that small effort seemed to weaken him.

"He is a man of means. It's not just that he could afford me. He didn't hesitate when I told him the size of my fee and didn't seem particularly surprised by it. I think that he already knew what the best cost and didn't hesitate to pay for it.

"He seemed so comfortable with the overall process, I'd say that he may be or had been engaged in some kind of illegal activity over a long period of time himself, though, of course, I can't be sure. Perhaps that's where he made his money? If so, I doubt that it was at the highest level. He has no self-awareness at all and thinks of himself as quite clever. If I had to guess, I'd say he worked independently, or perhaps as some sort of subcontractor.

"I sensed a strong element of revenge, too. His motive was entirely personal. When he spoke of you, it was with hatred. Perhaps that was the anger I heard. He didn't care one way or the other about your...about Dina. It was you he wanted to hurt for something done to him or someone close to him, I think, as if he was goaded by it every day of his life to the point of obsession.

"Our conversations had a strangely disjointed aspect, with long pauses as if he was waiting for something, thinking about what to say next, or digesting what I said. Perhaps he was just being cautious, but it seemed to be more and different than that."

He motioned for more water. I gave it to him, and once again, he drank it all.

"Most of what I extrapolated may be more instinctual

than factual, but my instincts were finely honed over many years and rarely wrong. You might be able to build on it and what other things I can tell you, especially if you're as good as you're supposed to be."

"How do you know how good I am?"

"I always look into the people around the target so that I can anticipate a response, if any. I realized that I had to be particularly careful in this case. I am never sloppy, but *if* I left even one small hint that this was not what it seemed to be, you and your friends, the Cabo San Lucas Police Chief, the wealthy skip tracer, and the one known as Chango would never have stopped looking. You wouldn't have found me. Until my desert collapse, no one ever came close. But you might have been nuisance enough to restrict my activity, which I could not abide for any length of time."

"I think you underestimate us," I said.

"Perhaps I do, or did," he admitted. "But, as I said before, it really doesn't matter now."

I stayed with him for more than three hours, until I couldn't think of anything else to ask. He was right, there were a lot of bits and pieces that might add up to something if I looked in the right places or turned over enough rocks. Or not.

To my surprise, he said that if he thought of anything more, he would find a way to get it to me. I could not imagine how, but I had no doubt that if anyone could do it, he could.

Was it enough to get me somewhere? I had no idea.

He was wearing down. His voice was weaker and the words came slower and with more effort as he seemed to sink deeper into the bed. Even the searing light from his blue eyes seemed to lessen, like his life force was fading.

I got up, folded the chair, and returned it to its original spot against the wall.

"It appears that we have come to the end," he said. "I enjoyed our conversation. I don't get many intelligent visitors, certainly not those ridiculous government drones. Their pomposity reeks like cheap cologne."

I didn't know what to say to that, so I didn't say anything.

"I won't insult your intelligence by saying I'm sorry. That would be absurd. You wouldn't believe me anyway.

"I didn't realize it until much too late, but doing what I did for so long had a corrosive effect. The dead should have their say, I think, and I have an almost over-whelming urge to let them. At this late date, I might as well give in to that urge, though I am usually careful not to incriminate my clients, unless they're dead, too. But in this case, it seemed...appropriate, I suppose. As I said, I didn't like the man.

"It's always difficult to assess one's own motives, but my revealing so many details about what I've done prob-ably is a way of having my say *before* I'm dead."

He offered, but I left the room without shaking his hand.

"I understand," he said, even though I didn't say anything.

CHAPTER 10

BURNSIDE and I were quiet as we walked back to his office, our steps echoing in the dreary hallway. I felt his curiosity, but decided not to satisfy it.

When we got to the office, Chango shot out of his chair and asked the burning question.

"Get anything?"

"Yeah, I got something," I replied. "I'm just not sure what, or if it'll be much of a help once I figure it out. It'll take a while to sort through everything."

As promised, Burnside quickly scanned my notes, nodded his approval at what he saw, and returned them. I turned over his notebook and cheesy pen. Chango and I recovered our belongings downstairs, shook hands with Burnside, vowed never to return, make contact in any way, or tell anyone we were here, and went on our way.

Neither Chango nor I said anything for most of the drive back to Santa Fe. I was caught up in my own thoughts, and Chango respected that.

As we got closer to town, after turning onto Old Santa Fe Trail and heading north to the hotel in a more or less straight shot, I broke the silence.

"You know, Chango, this is going to sound strange, but I kind of liked him."

From the driver's side, he shot me an unbelieving look.

"Cruickshank, you are truly fucking weird sometimes," he said. "You really are."

CHAPTER 11

WE HEADED BACK to Cabo the next morning.

As it did coming in, the drive to Albuquerque, turning in the rental car, waiting for more than an hour, the flight to the Dallas-Fort Worth airport, a two hour wait in the airline lounge, followed by the flight to Cabo and working our way out of that airport with all the tourists shot the hell out of the day.

Valencia and Heenan met us and Valencia drove to my condo. Desperately thirsty, I immediately cracked a *Bohemia* for myself, served up drinks to whoever wanted them, which was everybody, and we gathered in my living room for the postmortem. We could easily have been four guys sitting around with their feet on the coffee table, talking about the big game.

Consulting my notes, I went over everything the killer said, which took a while.

There were a few questions, which I answered as best I could, meaning that I didn't have many answers.

"Okay, so what can we do?" Heenan asked. "How can we help you out?"

"I've thought about that," I said, now deep into my

second beer. "The answer is nothing, at least not for right now."

They were pros, and no one looked surprised at an answer they knew was coming.

"I'm going to research my past cases, all the way back to the beginning," I explained. "I hope to enlist my computer geek's help. Maybe something will jog my memory. I dunno, maybe it won't be explicit in the files but it'll ring a bell. It'll be good to have two sets of eyes on it, too, but the whole thing is going to take a while."

Chango and Heenan were surprised that I had a computer geek, while Valencia seemed to know all about it.

"Please tell Ursula that if she has to get into my department's system for some reason, I'd appreciate it if she wouldn't break in this time," Valencia said, a smile crossing his lean face. "I will be happy to give her access. There is no reason for her to show off again. Everybody knows how good she is."

This time?

Again?

I didn't know that Valencia and Ursula knew each other, much less that he knew she worked for me, although once seen, Ursula *did* tend to linger in the memory. Plus there was very little going on in Cabo San Lucas that the chief *didn't* know, or at least suspect.

And while Valencia's comment implied that she'd already broken through the Cabo Police Department's digital security at least once, he didn't seem exactly devastated with concern.

Strange.

Chango and Heenan decided to fly home the next day. When I suggested there might be a problem finding seats on short notice, Heenan shrugged it away.

"It's wired, Ethan. Don't worry about it."

I later found out that he hired a private jet. No surprise there. That was just Heenan being Heenan.

Their leaving was almost as awkward as their arrival, which was only a few days ago but seemed like six weeks. I could tell that they didn't want to leave, but at the same time, knew there was no point in staying. I promised to keep them informed and ask for help if I needed it. They did not believe me.

Valencia took Chango and Heenan to their hotel, and suddenly I was alone. I needed to stay busy, so I called Maria at the office and set up an all-hands meeting early the next morning. Then I settled behind the desk in my home office, fired up the computer, and started transcribing the handwritten notes of my long interview with the assassin. It felt strange to keep calling him the assassin, if only in my head, but I couldn't think of anything better.

The notes took a long time to put together. There was a lot of information, and I had to be as precise and complete as possible. I didn't want something that I inadvertently added or misstated to shade or change the meaning of anything the assassin said and send Ursula off on a useless tangent, assuming she agreed to take this whole gnarly mess on.

By the time I finished and made several copies, I was pretty well shot. I took a quick shower and climbed into bed.

Fortunately I was reading a book, *Whalefall*, that provided plenty of escape considering it was a novel about a guy who was accidentally swallowed by an eighty-foot, sixty-ton sperm whale, gets pulled into the first of the whale's four stomachs, and only has one hour to escape before his oxygen tank runs out.

And I thought I had problems.

I didn't remember putting my Kindle aside or starting to fall asleep, but the next thing I knew, it was tomorrow.

CHAPTER 12

AS EXPECTED, everybody showed up for the morning meeting even if they had to rearrange their day.

Maria thoughtfully provided a big urn of coffee, which I welcomed because I felt a little fuzzy. The last few days took more out of me than I thought. The five of us made a crowd in our little conference room, but the meeting wouldn't last long. As far as I was concerned, the most productive meetings never did.

I watched as their faces changed from curiosity to surprise and finally anger as I explained what was going on, but without revealing how or where I got the information, which took a good bit of tap dancing on my part.

Mike Callahan's bulldog face turned skeptical, like a dark cloud passing across a grumpy sun. With his long experience as a Chicago Police Detective, he knew there was more to the story but didn't want to go after it—and me—in front of the others. I made a mental note to talk to him later.

When I finished, everybody started talking at once and I raised my hand to stop the babble.

"I know you want to help, and I appreciate it. But there isn't anything you can do right now. Besides, we can't just drop everything at the agency. The best move is to keep it going like nothing happened. I mean, everybody here likes getting paid, right? Maria can distribute my cases between Mike and Antonio. I do have a plan for the short term, but it doesn't require a lot of manpower."

And that was it. Mike and Antonio squeezed my shoulder on the way out, with Mike applying some extra oomph to signal that he knew I'd blown some smoke. Maria offered a supportive wink as she left to resume her position as chief dragon and gatekeeper.

As Ursula hefted her leather satchel over her shoulder, which always seemed to be bursting with paper and computer flotsam and jetsam, including an actual computer, I asked, "Could you stick around for a few minutes?"

She reversed course and gently settled the satchel on the next chair before stepping over to the urn to draw another cup of coffee. She motioned to ask if I wanted another cup. When I shook my head, she added two cubes of sugar and a little cream, stirred it, and plopped back in her chair.

"Ursula, if I remember correctly, we—and by we, I mean you—converted all of my old case files to digital, going all the way back to when I started in California. Once you caught up, you kept the files up to date so that we have print and digital versions of everything. Is that about right?"

"Yes, it is," she replied, casually brushing a strand of her long raven hair away from one eye. "The conversion was one of the first projects I did for you."

"And the paper files are still in the storage room?"

This time, she nodded without saying anything.

I pushed across the table a manila folder with the transcribed notes of my interview with the killer. She opened the folder and casually leafed through the notes while I explained what it was, what I wanted, and asked if she would keep it to herself for now.

"If whoever killed Dina comes from somewhere in my past, if possible, I want to find them by searching that past. I'm pretty sure it took more than a routine case to set all this in motion, so not every case needs a deep look. Most don't. But we need to take at least a casual look at everything. Maybe the law of unintended consequences was at work and something happened that we couldn't have predicted and didn't know at the time? That'll make it harder to find whatever the hell it is we're looking for, but I still want to try.

"Can you use your systems, procedures, programs, algorithms, or whatever you call that stuff, go through the digital files and come up with a list of possibilities? Like I said, I'd pay more attention to the major or unusual cases, at least on the first go-round. But don't restrict your search in any way. Go where it takes you.

"In the meantime, I'll do the same with the paper files. I know it'll be a lot slower, but it might trigger something in my memory. I have a connection with paper that I just don't have with digital. You know that better than anybody. When we're through, we can compare what we found and take a harder look at those high-probability cases our lists have in common.

"This is not an agency expense," I added. "It's personal. So make sure to give me the bill. I'm happy to pay as you go, all of it at the end, however you want."

I gave her a moment to think about it.

"Ursula, does all that blather make sense to you?"

Her reply was not what I expected.

"Ethan, you must know that I can't do what you ask."

Disappointment flooded through me like a riptide. I assumed she would be on board. The fact was that I needed her. How could I have misread it so badly?

"No, this is on me," she explained.

When I started to protest, she stopped me cold.

"Tell me, do you think Valencia and your other friends will send you a bill?"

She lifted her chin to take in the agency's office and the people in it.

"And if they get a chance to help, do you think anybody here will be so insulting as to hand you an invoice? Ethan Cruickshank, do you really think so little of us? Of me?"

She added something in her native Portuguese, a language I never understood and never would, but the meaning was clear: *Don't be such a numb nuts, Cruickshank.*

"I know exactly what you want, you silly goose. You're right in that it will take you much longer, but research from different points of view is a good idea as long as we have the same goal."

After that spasm of disappointment, I found myself sighing with relief, like I'd been holding my breath for a couple of days. Ursula's help was critical.

"That reminds me, Valencia said if you need information from his department, he'd appreciate it if you wouldn't break into the system again. He's happy to provide access. I couldn't help but wonder what he meant by *again*."

Another miracle smile. "Last year, a few months before I began working with you, he asked me for an analysis of the police department's digital security. It was badly needed. The system was probably twenty years old and security was so primitive that any computer-savvy ten-year-old could break in."

"Which these days means most ten-year-olds," I said

She took a sip of her coffee, which by now had to be lukewarm at best.

"I did as he asked and offered my thoughts along

with several strong suggestions in a report, volunteering to make the improvements myself. When I didn't hear back, without telling Valencia, I tested to see if anything had been done by breaking into the system. It still was pathetically easy.

"It wasn't hard to find out why. Embarrassed by my report, especially coming from a mere *woman*, the so-called *policia* experts acted on only the easiest and most obvious of my recommendations, while claiming they diligently followed through on everything and even improved on it, taking care of problems they claimed that I carelessly missed in my rush to impress Valencia."

"In other words, they lied to cover their butts and boot you out of the picture at the same time," I said.

"Not in other words, Ethan. Those *are* the words."

She took another sip of coffee, made a face, and set the cup aside. "The ease with which I got in the second time, and the mocking signs I left behind, was humiliating for those people. I made sure of that, just as I made sure Valencia knew exactly what happened. After a bit of time, certain heads rolled, fewer but better heads replaced them, and Valencia's department is stronger for it."

"You probably made a few enemies, too, something to keep in mind down the line," I said. "I didn't know that you and Valencia knew each other."

"Oh, yes," she said. "Very well."

There was something there, something in her eyes, the hint of a smile, a slight softening in attitude. Whatever it was hit me like somebody dropped a safe on my head. I felt like Wile E. Coyote losing another round to the Roadrunner.

"Are you two…are you…you are aren't you!"

"Yes," she said with a wry smile. "I suppose we are."

And I was one surprised PI.

Because she worked with the agency so frequently, I

usually saw Ursula at least once a week. And Valencia was my closest friend in Cabo San Lucas, or anywhere, for that matter, despite our getting off on the wrong foot years ago when he slapped a hammerlock on me as a prelude to arrest.

Like Bogart said to Claude Rains in *Casablanca*, it was the start of a beautiful friendship.

And yet I didn't have a clue what was going on right under my nose.

Why not? Because they kept their private lives private.

Why shouldn't they?

And why did I think it was any of my business?

I am a nosy bastard, that's why. I'm a private investigator, not an appliance salesman.

"It's not that we're embarrassed or anything like it," Ursula said, though I could tell she didn't like talking about it. "Such feelings would be ridiculous. We just don't want gossip and the attention that comes with it to complicate our lives.

"As you know, to the puzzlement of many in high places, Valencia has several times refused more prestigious law enforcement positions, including high up in the federal government. Oddly enough, his reluctance put him in even greater demand.

"But at the same time, he is regarded with suspicion in some quarters because they do not understand him. He is known throughout Mexico as a rising star, or would be if only he would stop refusing to rise."

"You're becoming pretty well known, too," I said. "You hardly fit the IT stereotype, and your competence is beyond anything I've ever seen. You two make quite the pair."

I couldn't help myself.

"So tell me. Is it serious?"

She could have told me to mind my own damn business, and she would have been right, but settled instead for a mild scold.

"When I said *get in our way,* I meant intrusive questions such as that," she said, her eyes narrowing. "We don't know how serious we are, or if we're serious at all, and shouldn't have to explain it to anyone. For now, Valencia and I are just enjoying the moment."

She gave me a level look, a sign that I had pushed her as far as she would go.

"Ethan, can I trust you to say nothing?

"Not a word," I said. "But it might be best if you tell Valencia that I know, so that I'll know that he knows that I know…and, well, you know?"

"If I understand what you are trying to say, I will tell him so you can avoid pretending not to know. It could be awkward."

"Yeah," I said. "Kind of like right now."

CHAPTER 13

I SPENT MORE than an hour carrying plastic file boxes from our office storage room down to my SUV in the parking lot. Even with the back seat down, the boxes filled the SUV almost to the roof, with more in the front seat.

It took even longer than that to carry all the boxes from the underground garage at the condo up to my home office. By the time I finished, I was sweating like a farmer who spent the day plowing hard ground behind a stubborn mule.

Detective work is so glamorous.

I drove an SUV because I didn't know what to do after my classic '65 Mustang was killed by the hurricane that almost did me in, too. As much as I loved the Mustang, it was not a great car for a PI. It attracted too much attention and was easy to spot on a tail.

Like what seemed like half the population of Cabo, I bought a white SUV. I soon regretted my decision. The SUV was so boring that just thinking about it made me drowsy. On the other hand, moving the file boxes in the smaller Mustang would have taken at least a couple of trips and a lot more time.

And so passed eight days of my life I'll never get back.

It took a while to find the rhythm of the research. At first, I got caught up in a nostalgia-fest. Some cases I remembered well, others only vaguely, and a few not at all. Memories had a way of dredging up other memories until I'd look at my watch and wonder where the hell the last forty-five minutes went.

That would never do. I didn't want to make this a lifetime project. So I brought more discipline to the process, or tried to. I followed my own advice and dismissed most of the minor cases quickly. Background checks and insurance claims? Forget it. Simple missing person cases, like runaway kids-husbands-wives who were easily found? Never mind. Divorces where both sides wanted out and nobody really needed a PI in the first place? Outta here.

Even those eliminations left a lot of paper to work through. Shuffling my way through it case by case took time and attention to detail. As time passed, I felt like a lowly scrivener laboring to translate a religious tract from its original Aramaic.

I took three breaks over eight days. Two afternoons, I went down to the condo pool, where I swam laps until I thought my arms and legs might fall off. Another afternoon, I worked out for an hour in the condo gym. It was good to know there was other life and other things to do on the planet.

I set up three categories for those cases that made the cut—strong, medium, and possible. By the time I finished, I had four in the strong category, with the right mix of importance, emotion, and circumstance, and fifteen total in my three categories. The rest I dismissed as unlikely.

It was time to have another talk with Ursula, who'd probably finished and moved on to a new career by now.

CHAPTER 14

To keep the investigation as private as possible, we met at my place, spreading everything out on my dining room table.

As I expected, it only took Ursula a couple of days to complete her research. The good news was that, with three exceptions, we came up with virtually the same list.

We were only a few minutes into it when someone called: Chango. I took the call. From him, I always did.

"I just heard that your friend Nathan died last night."

I'd spent so much time rummaging around in my past that it took a moment before I remembered who Nathan was—the assassin. The only name any of us knew him by was the phony name on the phony ID he had on him when they found him half dead in the New Mexico desert—Nathan Brittles.

I knew the man was dying, but it still was a shock to hear that he did. The depth of all that I felt was like a pot brought to a sudden boil.

"You there?" Chango asked into the silence.

"Yeah."

"Even though Nathan's dead, obviously our friend

who told me about it is being careful," Chango said. "We should continue to respect that."

Chango was telling me not to try to contact Don Burnside, the New Mexico State pen warden, although I couldn't imagine why I would want to.

"I get it," I said. "It's just a strange feeling, like I never really thought he would die, even though I knew better."

"I've said this before, a lot, but you complicate things too much," Chango said. "But that's the way you are and everybody who knows you has to live with you being a pain in the ass sometimes. Anyway, I hope you got everything out of him you needed because you're sure as hell not going to get anything more."

It turned out that even Chango could be wrong.

CHAPTER 15

URSULA and I spent the next three hours side by side going over the cases, searching for some sign that we were on the right track, or a way to get on the right track. I was sure it was there somewhere.

The problem was that we still didn't have enough information to know what we didn't know. I felt like we were going in circles and making a little progress at the same time.

Maybe the circle was drawing tighter?

Maybe we really were making progress?

Maybe I was losing my mind?

Ursula had an appointment with another client and I needed a break, so we decided to meet again the next day.

Eager to get out of my own head, I drove into town, parking in one of the spots we rented in a lot near the agency. Parking on the street in Cabo San Lucas could be next to impossible, especially during the high season when it was winter almost everywhere else and the town was loaded with tourists, their rental cars, and their lousy driving. It wasn't a very efficient use of time for anybody at the agency to spend half an hour searching for a place to park, so I made it easy and rented a few spots long-term.

I had no plan other than an easy stroll around town, which was one of my favorite things to do in Cabo. Where others might see a lot of tacky shops selling everything from bottles of tequila you could get anywhere, to serapes made in China, and Cuban cigars that have never been to Cuba, I saw life in all its mad glory, full of people who were just trying to get by from one day to the next, and not waiting for somebody or something to take care of them, all the while keeping their sense of humor.

I knew that despite the popular boast of *almost free* for whatever they were selling, they reliably screwed the tourists with almost every transaction. But isn't that what tourists are for?

I ambled around the marina with the boat slips to my right, jammed with everything from floating mansions worth a hundred million dollars or more to tiny *pangas*, popular little workhorse craft used for everything from fishing to water taxis.

On my left was what seemed like an unending array of open-front bars and restaurants touting every cuisine you could imagine, along with a few that were unimaginable. At night, as the crowds thickened, employees, and sometimes the managers or owners, stationed themselves outside the restaurants, waving plastic-coated menus like they were bringing in approaching aircraft, collaring passersby with promises of great deals—*almost free* again —and unspeakable gastronomic delight, along with coupons offering free or discounted margaritas or tequila shots guaranteed to lubricate the wallet. They were lucky if one in a hundred passersby said yes, or even stopped to listen to the pitch before moving on.

Some people, especially first-timers in Cabo, claimed to be repelled by the scene and demanded something more authentic, whatever that meant. I understood that point of view without agreeing with it. To me, it was entertaining, almost a kind of street theater. What could be more authentic than somebody out on a crowded sidewalk hustling their business against impossible odds night after night?

I stopped at a bar owned by a big-bellied character named Fred Augustine, whose wife dumped him three or four years ago. He still didn't understand why, which probably went far to explain why she dumped him.

Needing a change, Fred didn't hold back. He sold his two Jersey City paint stores, reduced his possessions to everything he could fit in one suitcase, moved to Cabo, and bought the little bar when the longtime owner retired. After spending all of about five hundred bucks turning the place into a cheesy imitation of a tiki bar, to his surprise, he made a lot more money than he ever did selling paint in New Jersey.

Thanks to my small portion of celebrity, he always comped me when I stopped in for a drink, which is one reason why I occasionally stopped in for a drink, took my ease at the long mahogany bar, and watched the parade pass by.

Also, while I mostly liked Fred, bar owners and tenders can be good sources for what's going on around town, the kind of thing official Cabo might never hear, or want to.

Without bothering to ask, he poured my usual and set it on the bar at my elbow—Black Bush Irish Whiskey on the rocks. I was pretty sure he kept the Black Bush in stock just for me.

"Been a while since you were around, Ethan," he said, his beefy arms forearms down on the bar. "What's up, my man?"

I shrugged, took a sip of my drink, nodded to show my satisfaction, and set it down on the bar.

"Fred, despite what a lot of people think, I am usually the last one to know."

Fred smiled his best, knowing smile. He thought I was being modest.

CHAPTER 16

ONE DRINK WAS ENOUGH. I wanted to get out of my head, not pickle it in alcohol.

I walked back to the SUV, climbed in, took a moment to savor the vehicle's dullness, cranked it up, and drove home.

I stopped at the condo lobby to pick up my mail, took the elevator up to my place, and settled into a chair on the balcony to go through the usual junk, which I long ago found was just as voluminous in Mexico as it was in the US.

One small envelope stood out from the rest. My address was handwritten across the front in pencil with no return address. The postmark was Sioux Falls, Iowa. I was pretty sure that I didn't know anyone in Sioux Falls, or all of Iowa, for that matter. I couldn't even prove there *was* an Iowa.

Inside was a single sheet of paper, folded precisely into thirds. I unfolded it to reveal a name I didn't know and several sentences in shaky but clear handwriting.

> Rudy O'Bannion
> I am afraid that I wasn't as truthful with

you as I might have been. A lifetime of deceit will do that. I didn't give you this name when we talked, and I realize now that I should have. I didn't lie. This is not the name of my client, but it is a name you should find useful. Any successful hunt requires a trail to follow, however faint.

Don't bother trying to trace this note, though I can't think of a reason why you would want to. The postmark means nothing except misdirection for anyone who might be interested but shouldn't be. It doesn't matter because by the time you read this, I will be dead. But, as I told you, if you're as good as I think you are...

Nathan

Even in death, he was still pulling the strings. I had no idea how a dying man managed to get the note to me from the state pen in New Mexico with a Sioux Falls postmark.

But however he did it, a voice from the grave just showed me the way.

CHAPTER 17

BEFORE I COULD THINK about what to do next, I was surprised by a call from Ursula.

She didn't often make contact by something as primitive as the telephone, preferring texts, iMessages, and other ways I didn't even know existed. To her, email was as primitive as a Western Union telegram was to me. But she knew me well enough to know that I could go several days before I figured out that I had something as simple as an instant message waiting, and then spend more time puzzling over how to get to it.

"Ethan, we're being watched, at least somebody's trying to."

"Excuse me?"

"Someone is trying to spy on us. I just found it. They must be good or I would have discovered it sooner."

"By 'being watched' and 'spy on us' you mean what, exactly?"

"Someone is trying to get access to your computer, pad, and cell phone. It looks like they started a couple days ago. They tried to get to Valencia, too. Fortunately, I already created protection that is virtually impossible to break unless the best in the world with unlimited time and resources worked on it non-stop for a week, and even then, it would be difficult.

"Some time ago, I gave roughly the same protection to Valencia's personal information, to you, and to your agency. I am pleased to say that it worked. Whoever is trying to get in was stopped exactly where they were supposed to be stopped. They tried your friend Heenan, too, but with no success, I can see. He must have his own excellent security. I have nothing on Suarez."

"That's because there's nothing to find. I doubt that Chango could turn on a computer, much less own one. He wouldn't know Facebook from a facial."

"He must have a pad or cell phone."

"No pad. I saw him try a pad once and he wound up throwing it against the wall. He uses his cell phone about once a month, if that, and even then, he uses a burner, but only if there's no other choice. He is the last guy I know who still uses pay phones. I think he knows the location of every pay phone in the country. If he absolutely has to, sometimes he'll make a call on somebody else's phone."

"My God! He's even worse than you are."

"Much worse, as hard as that is to believe," I agreed. "I assume this is related to what we're doing?"

"Of course, why else would someone want to spy on all of us?"

"If you try to find out who it is, or where it's coming from, will they know?"

There was silence while she thought it over.

"If I am too aggressive and heavy-handed, almost certainly," she said. "I probably can find out, but subtlety takes more time and care. How much time, I cannot say."

"In that case, don't do anything," I said. "At least nothing they're likely to see."

"Really?"

"If they don't know that we know, we might be able

to use that against them sometime down the road," I explained. "You're sure they're not successfully spying on us in any way?"

"I'm sure, but I will keep watching and take measures if I have to. They will never know."

"I have some burners at the office. Go get one...and one for Valencia, too. Tell Maria I okayed it. I assume you'll see Valencia pretty soon."

"Tonight," she said.

"Okay, tell him about all this then."

"What about Suarez and Heenan?"

"I'm not worried about Chango, though I'll let him know. I can back door Heenan to warn him, though I'd appreciate it if you'd keep checking on them, too, as best you can."

Heenan used burners all the time, at least for his personal use, changing every few days. He also had an old-school rotary telephone made of old-school Bakelite with a dedicated line at his beach home in Southern California.

Heenan liked old things. He also owned a big 1950s era Wurlitzer jukebox with so many colorful flashing lights it looked like a carnival while it played actual forty-five rpm records in pristine condition. He once bragged that he had more than a thousand old forty-fives.

The first time I saw him use the big black rotary phone, I joked that he looked like Humphrey Bogart in *The Maltese Falcon*, only without the fedora. He was so pleased with the image that he preened in the mirror and followed it up with the world's worst Bogart impersonation. I told him that if he ever did that again I'd shoot him in the leg.

I told Ursula about the name Rudy O'Bannion, though not revealing where and how I got it to keep

Burnside in the clear. I had full confidence in Ursula, but a promise is a promise. I told her to tell Valencia, too. As police chief, he had access to law enforcement information all over the world, especially Interpol, where he used to work, and might be able to run down the name.

Contacting Heenan. I explained the situation and asked him to check out the name with whatever sources he had. Heenan probably knew more unsavory characters than any of us. A lot of people thought that he was pretty unsavory.

I called a couple of other contacts in Southern California, too. One guy was a lieutenant with the Los Angeles Police Department. The other, a woman I worked with many years ago on a case, was a PI with a large agency in San Diego. Both of them were experienced, reliable, and not the type to blow smoke just to seem important. I didn't hope for much, but you never know.

I debated contacting Chango. I knew that he'd help, of course, but I'd leaned on him enough for now.

I couldn't get used to the idea, but Chango Suarez was no longer a young man. Hell, it had been a long time since he was a young man. It was past time for me to break away from the mother ship for a while and let him live his own life. He'd earned it more than anyone I knew.

Going through my case files, it took a while to find what I was looking for. The name O'Bannion was in a file that ranked at the bottom the list of possibilities. Ursula had the same case just as far off her radar, too.

After throwing out all the lines I had, it finally looked like there might be something on the hook, or at least swimming in that direction.

CHAPTER 18

DESPITE THIS OUTBREAK of something that looked suspiciously like progress, the next morning I had to break off and drive to San Jose del Cabo to give a deposition related to a case the agency worked on several months ago.

A single mother who recently moved to San Jose from suburban Philadelphia after an ugly divorce was afraid that her rebellious fifteen-year-old son was hanging out with a bad crowd. She asked if I could look into it without letting her son know.

An Anglo named Ethan Cruickshank, whose Spanish was awkward at best, was not a good fit for the job, but it was perfect for Antonio, who was local and a lot closer to the right age to blend in. At the time, he was on the agency's six-month probation period for new employees, and this was his first real case.

Maria was right to warn me that it was a risk putting him out there alone, but even that early, I had faith in the young man. I was interested to see how he'd do in the field, where supervision was of necessity loose.

Antonio performed as well as anyone could, getting everything we—and our client—needed and more. To his delight and my satisfaction, I immediately ended his probation and brought him into the agency with no strings attached.

It turned out that the mother had a right to be worried. Her son hadn't done anything wrong, yet, but he certainly would if he continued down the road he was on.

After going over Antonio's findings after he shadowed the kid for a couple of weeks, I suggested that the mother turn the whole thing over to the San Jose del Cabo Police, which she did after I guided her to the right people and made a few calls to help ease her way.

When the police promised to keep her son out of it, I gave them everything we had on what amounted to a new but still loosely formed gang in the making.

The cops in San Jose already knew the gang pretty well, down to the meaning of their stupid tattoos and gang signs. But the department didn't have the manpower to follow anybody for a couple of weeks and gather evidence like Antonio did.

Armed with the information we provided, they were so eager to pounce that they were too aggressive, catching a couple of innocent teenagers in the rough and indiscriminate roundup. It was a perfect example of being in the wrong place at the wrong time.

Though Mexico wasn't nearly as litigious as the United States, the parents of the kids caught in the net found an attorney with the attitude of a starving shark and sued the city and police department for the usual fortune. The department not only proclaimed its innocence, it hinted that the young people might not be as innocent as their parents believed them to be, an allegation that was as stupid as it was untrue. It infuriated the parents even more than they already were, and now both sides wanted a deposition from the agency.

I trust Antonio, but depositions can be tricky, and this kind of thing was beyond his experience. Since I owned the agency and was ultimately responsible for everything it did, after consulting with our own attorney, it was agreed by all parties that I should be the one to give the deposition.

Once tempers cooled, I was confident that everything would be worked out before the case got to court, assuming the police department groveled sufficiently and wrote a satisfying check.

At worst, I'd figured that I'd spend a couple of hours talking to a room full of lawyers. That might give me cooties, but nothing worse.

Which only proves that sometimes I don't know what I'm talking about.

CHAPTER 19

IT WAS the usual perfect spring day in Los Cabos, with a nice middling temperature neither too hot nor too cold and golden sunlight reflecting off the water in a way that made you feel strong, healthy, and invincible.

Instead of taking the newer and smoother inland highway connecting Cabo San Lucas with San Jose del Cabo, I opted for the old coast road, which was the only direct route between the two towns when we first came down from Southern California. It was slower, and parts of it weren't in great condition, but it was a drive I enjoyed, with beautiful views and reasonable traffic.

Unfortunately, with so many resorts going up along the beachfront corridor between the two Cabos, water views from the highway were rapidly diminishing. But a few spots here and there still offered reminders of why we moved here in the first place.

One long curving section a few miles outside of San Jose del Cabo overlooked a beach that used to be much favored by surfers, many of them down from the US. They'd camp on the beach at night, complete with bonfires, marijuana, beer, and cheap wine, until the cops ran them off, which they rarely did unless someone complained. The scene resembled a 1960s flashback. Now, with everything going upscale, such things rarely happened anymore, and in my opinion, Los Cabos was worse for it.

I had plenty of time and was in no hurry. Driving slightly under the speed limit, I floated along in the right lane to savor the occasional view overlooking beach and sea.

My peaceful day blew to pieces in just a few seconds.

Caught up in memories of how it used to be and cruising on the mental automatic pilot that all good drivers possess, as I rounded the long curve over what used to be the surfer's beach, a 1990s-era American sedan barreled up on my left, its ancient engine racing with bad intentions as it cut hard toward my SUV.

I was lucky the driver was no expert. A pro would have passed me miles back, then slowed down and cut me off from the front instead of racing up from the rear. Relaxed and enjoying the drive, I might not have paid much attention until I was in trouble.

The rattling noise from the overworked engine as the sedan moved alongside made me look toward the source of the racket. I didn't like what I saw.

The sedan crashed hard against the left front quarter of my SUV with the intent of running me off the road, where the driver figured that I'd take a fifteen or twenty-foot drop to the sand that would not be good for my health.

I stomped on the brakes. The other driver was slow to react, and suddenly the sedan was more than a length ahead. As it passed, I hit the gas, turned sharp to the left, and slid around in back of the sedan. Moving fast, I turned to the right so that now I was ahead on his left and in good position to run *him* off the road.

Which I did, with a screech of tortured metal and

smoking tires as the old sedan lurched in a direction it didn't want to go. The driver either didn't think to hit the brakes or panicked and tried to steer the big, sloppy car out of trouble, but with nowhere to go.

He also forgot to do his homework.

If he'd checked the site earlier, something any pro would do, he would have found a temporary cement barrier about three feet high and five or six feet off the road. After too many accidents, it was installed just a few days earlier to keep careless or drunk drivers from sailing off the macadam, particularly at night after a high old time in Cabo San Lucas. I heard about it from Maria, who made the drive once or twice a week to visit her sister and her family in San Jose.

Without slowing down, the sedan hit the barrier with an explosive crash that could have been heard in Mexico City. The front of the old car crumpled like an accordion. As I came to a screeching stop, in my rearview mirror, I saw the driver's airbag deploy. It hit him hard enough to knock off his Joe Cool mirrored sunglasses so they were hanging from one ear. The airbag trapped him in the car and possibly broke a rib or two. At least I hoped so.

After lingering behind the wheel for a moment to take a few deep breaths and let the adrenaline rush pass, I released my death grip on the steering wheel, got out of the SUV, and cautiously approached the wreck, my legs still a little wobbly.

I had a gun in the glove compartment and a permit to carry from Valencia, but I didn't want to get the weapon out because the *policia* would be here any minute and I didn't want the hassle.

It didn't matter. The driver was trapped behind the wheel by the airbag so that it looked like he was pinned by a giant marshmallow.

Two other cars, whose drivers saw what happened

without knowing why, stopped to help. Since there was nothing anyone could do, a half dozen of us stood around looking at the mess. Hot water from the sedan's crushed radiator hissed and steamed, releasing clouds of vapor while the old car leaked the rest of its fluids on the asphalt in a vile shade of green.

I did not know the first San Jose del Cabo patrolman who responded, a young uniformed cop who tried to seem older and more experienced by copping an attitude.

Bursting with self-importance, he bounded out of his car and started barking orders to establish his authority. I didn't mind the bluster. It's better to start hard and back off if warranted than to go in soft and then try to get the edge. The second way rarely works. Once initiative is lost, it's almost impossible to get it back. I just let him bark and feel good about himself.

I did know the second cop, who rattled up in the same old rattletrap of an unmarked car he'd driven for years. A plainclothes veteran with so many years of seniority he must have joined the force before the young patrolman was born, Manuel Ortega wasn't entirely honest and everyone knew it, but he also kept that dishonesty within the limits of his own peculiar code. Ortega was a good cop, and everyone knew that, too.

Manny had put on so much weight since I last saw him, it was almost painful to watch as he struggled to get out of his car with a lot of huffing and puffing. With an unlit cigar that might have cost as much as ten pesos anchored between the fingers of one hand, he surveyed the damage like a grandee assessing his estate, taking special note of the tire marks on the road.

Assessment completed, he ordered the young cop to take photos of the site, especially the tire marks and damage to both vehicles. He did, but not happily. The younger man's attitude made it obvious that he thought the task beneath him.

Having established his authority without raising his voice, Manny waddled over and offered his usual sarcastic greeting in heavily accented English.

"*Hola*, if it isn't *Etan Crankshift*, the world-famous detective to the stars."

It's hard to believe, but many Mexicans had trouble with my name. So did many English speakers.

Or, as in Manny's case, sometimes they just acted like it if they wanted to yank my chain.

"I see that you still have your usual light touch," he said, vastly amused at his own wit. "So tell me, *amigo*, what have you done to interrupt my pleasant day?"

Sirens blaring, the EMTs showed up and began extricating the driver from the clutches of his wrecked sedan while I explained what happened.

When I finished my story, after asking a few questions and listening intently to my answers for any inconsistencies, Manny sighed as if all the burdens of the world had settled around his sloping shoulders.

"So you are saying that you don't know and have never seen this man who you claim tried to run you off the road? And as far as you recall, there are no unpaid creditors or over-charged clients in your past seeking revenge, at least none that you know about?"

When I affirmed his conclusion, Manny slowly shook his head, showing great sorrow at the way the world constantly let him down.

"*Etan*, I must tell you that what you say very much strains my…uh…how do I put it?"

"Manny, I can only imagine what it strains. I hope it doesn't hurt. And I'm happy to see that you're still a funny guy after all these years," I said. "But at the risk of repeating myself, I can only say that I've never seen this character before, and I really don't know what this was all about.

"By the way, I'm fine. Thanks for asking."

Actually, I had a pretty good idea what just happened and why. But this was not the time or place to spill my guts.

CHAPTER 20

IT TOOK ALMOST two hours to sort everything out.

It could have been worse. Everything was handled on site and I didn't have to go to the *policia* station in San Jose. My SUV had serious dings and scrapes along both sides, but it was drivable. It may be boring, but it's sturdy as hell.

After telling the police what they saw, which supported my own story, the witnesses left their names and numbers with Manny, who appeared even more troubled by the foibles of humanity, as if he'd already seen everything there was to see and heard everything there was to hear and wished somebody would change the tune.

I knew he was posing, and he knew that I knew it, but he did it well. It was a performance we both enjoyed.

The wrecked sedan was towed away, probably to be turned into a metal cube in a junkyard somewhere, and the driver taken away, presumably to the hospital, with the young cop dutifully following in his patrol car.

One of the EMTs said that the driver probably had at least one broken rib. I knew how much that could hurt with every breath and struggled to keep my smile to myself.

After a few minutes back in his car, wedged behind the steering wheel while he talked to headquarters and stifled yawns, Manny revealed that the sedan was reported stolen north of Los Cabos in La Paz two days ago. He had an ID on the driver, too, though he refused to share it with me.

"It is much too early," he said. "Our investigation has barely begun, and it is not my job to feed you information so that you can start your own."

Manny lowered his sunglasses so he could give me a hard look over the top.

"*Senior, Etan Crankshaft*, I think you know more than you are telling me. This does not make me happy. You know very well that information is a two-way street."

"Manny, it does sort of look like our two-way street has come to a dead end," I agreed. "It must be shattering for an idealistic young man like yourself. But what makes you think I'm holding back information? What good would that do?"

Lighting his moist cigar with a wooden match that he flicked to flame with his thumbnail, Manny responded with a shrug.

"Because you always do," he said, blowing out the match. "I am sure your friend Valencia will find out everything you want to know anyway, along with many other things that you should not know. Unfortunately, there is nothing I can do about that."

"Valencia does what Valencia does."

I sounded like I was reading a fortune cookie.

After taking my leave of Manny, I called to explain why I didn't make my deposition this morning. All those lawyers would just have to wait.

No cooties today.

CHAPTER 21

"Four thousand dollars! That's ridiculous!"

"And here I thought you would be flattered," chuckled Valencia. "Is it possible that I am wrong?"

We were in Valencia's tiny office at the Cabo Police Station. It was immaculate, as usual, but with the desk, his chair, a visitor's chair, and a metal filing cabinet with a coffee maker gurgling on top, there was barely enough room for the two of us.

With Valencia twisting every arm he could reach, the police department had added a lot of manpower during his reign and outgrew its headquarters. The old building was so crowded that he voluntarily gave up his large office for this much smaller one, insisting that that was all he needed. Like me, he wasn't in the office much and wasn't interested in the trappings of power. A trusted assistant handled most of the paperwork.

Between sips of his ever-present coffee out of a white mug, Valencia said that the guy who tried to run me off the road was paid four grand for the job, information that he seemed to find amusing.

That made one of us.

"Peanuts!" I grumped. "Chump change!"

"If it makes you feel better, it may have started at at least double that as it passed down the line until someone stupid enough to do the job for so little was found, with everyone taking a cut as it passed through their hands," Valencia explained.

"How the hell would that work?" I asked. "It sounds like the village idiot's way to do business."

"It's a con, of course," he said. "The first contact claims to know someone who can do the job and says he will make the connection for a finder's fee. The second contact says the same thing, probably clued in by the first man. Everybody runs their own little scam until they find some fool who will do it for so little.

"It is also possible that it stopped with the first man, who kept most of the money for himself and paid the rest to the world's most incompetent killer."

"That's still low rent," I growled. "Where'd they find this character, aisle ten at Walmart?"

"That may be giving him too much credit," Valencia said. "However, there is something unusual about the whole thing that might be important to us."

"Yeah, I know," I said. "The price difference."

I was over the mostly feigned unhappiness with the bargain basement contract on my life. As long as I was still among the living, what did it matter?

Valencia followed the thread. "I see two possibilities. Perhaps different people…"

"Or the same person used someone else's money the first time, with Dina, and their own money with me," I said. "There's a hell of a difference between well over a million dollars and eight thousand or so, if that's where it started, the cheap bastard."

"The attempt on your life was remarkably sloppy, everything from the payment to how the deed was done," Valencia agreed. "It displays all the difference between amateurs and professionals, or between stupid and smart. Or, as I said, perhaps there were different people involved for different reasons?"

So far, this line of thinking didn't exactly narrow the range of possibilities.

The timing was something to consider, too.

I half expected somebody to take a run at me sometime. That was the reason I got involved in this thing in the first place, at least that's what I told myself.

But the attempt on my life happened so soon after my conversation with the assassin in the New Mexico penitentiary that someone must have been afraid that he talked and felt that they had to make their move quickly.

Or maybe they weren't afraid that he talked? Maybe they *knew* it. That might be a better explanation for such a fast—if bungling—response.

Whoever ordered the hit on me, it might be cheap and stupid, but they weren't indecisive.

But how did they know the assassin was even in custody, let alone where he was held? Did somebody with the Feebs break the security that was supposed to be so tight?

The obvious answer was yes. It happened when his friend with the big mouth blabbed to Chango, so why not someone else, or even the same guy?

But the Feebs weren't supposed to know that I talked to the assassin. And if they didn't know, then the list of who might have talked was a short one, and I'd known and trusted all but one of them for years.

Valencia waited patiently behind his desk, sipping his coffee while I thought out loud, trying to sort through it all.

When I finished, he responded with a theatrical sigh. "My friend, this case is making my head hurt."

"No kidding," I said. "I feel like we're going every which way but forward."

The oaf who tried to run me off the road was no help. He claimed that he didn't know anything except the first name of the man who offered him the job, which he knew wasn't his real name anyway. His description—average height, dark hair, slim—fit half the Mexican males between puberty and old age.

They met at a bar, he said.

It was strictly a cash transaction, he said, with a thousand dollars before and the rest to be paid after.

No, he'd never seen him before, he said.

Now he wished he never had, he said.

And by the way, he was really sorry and promised never to do anything like it again, he said.

Could he go home now?

Everyone who knew this clown believed that he really was as ignorant as he claimed. Valencia described him as a notorious low-life doofus well-known around southern Baja who was regarded as too stupid to fake ignorance and too much of a bottom-feeder to know that four thousand dollars wasn't big money. To him, it was probably the biggest payday of his miserable life.

Valencia dismissed him as *mierda de la calle*, which translated as "street shit."

I had to agree after watching a recording in Valencia's office of the interrogation by the San Jose del Cabo *Policia*, led by good old Manny, who dropped his world-weary pose for a healthy dose of fire and brimstone.

The interrogation stopped short of using an old-school rubber hose, but not that much short. It was obvious that the guy's ribs were hurting from the crash. It turned out that Manny ordered the ambulance to take the patient to the police station, not the hospital. The emergency guys protested that Manny was forcing them to break the law, but he was not moved by their plea.

After about ninety seconds of bravado, it was obvious that if he knew anything the would-be killer would have spilled it like water from a bucket, especially after Manny *accidentally* gave him a hard forearm in the vicinity of his damaged ribs and then planted him in the metal folding chair like he was driving a stake into the ground with his bare hands. Even with the low-quality video, I could see the poor sap shaking with pain and fear.

At least Manny enjoyed himself. At one point, he looked at the camera and winked.

The San Jose del Cabo Police tried following the money trail, but lost it when it went north into the western US and disappeared, along with most of their interest.

"Are we gonna get any help at all from north of the border?" I asked.

I shouldn't have bothered.

"We will grow old waiting, and I don't blame them," Valencia said. "An attempted murder in a foreign country where no one was hurt except the would-be killer and where the small amount of money involved may or may not have come from somewhere in the western US will not rank high on their things-to-do list."

"There's something else that's interesting," I said, hiking my feet up on Valencia's desk and crossing my ankles.

It wasn't very comfortable, just my way of getting revenge for Valencia's amusement about the low-rent price on my life. Maturity is my middle name. After I left, the meticulous police chief would probably order somebody in full hazmat gear to come in and power wash the desktop.

"The assassin told me that based on some unintentionally dropped references, he was pretty sure the guy who contacted him lived somewhere in the mountain or western time zones of the US," I explained.

"He said that he didn't seem very bright, too, which fits the attempt on me. Like you said, it's impossible to get good help on a rush job with bargain basement wages. Anybody with an IQ higher than a mudslide would know that. From start to finish, the whole thing was not a work of brilliance."

Valencia raised his eyebrows while warily watching my feet on his desk. Multi-tasking at its best.

"Yeah, I know, we're rocketing along," I said. "Just sitting here in your luxurious office while you drink coffee we cut the possibilities down to all the stupid people in two time zones and umpteen states."

"*Madre de Dios*, this thing is practically solving itself," Valencia said, with a smite to his forehead.

There were a couple of other things I didn't mention. I wanted to take a good look at both of them before getting everybody excited.

If I remembered correctly, the case involving the name O'Bannion originated in Northern California. That was the only thing I did remember about it.

And I was beginning to wonder about Don Burnside, the well-dressed warden of Santa Fe.

CHAPTER 22

WITHOUT TELLING HER WHY, I asked Ursula to take a look at Burnside, especially his financials.

Other than Valencia, Chango, and Heenan, Burnside was the only one who knew that I'd talked to the assassin and took pains to keep it that way.

Or so he said.

While I didn't know that he was dirty, I didn't not know it either. The more I thought about it, the more I didn't like what I was thinking. Maybe I'd have to contact Chango after all and find out how well he really knew Don Burnside.

I settled behind the desk in my home office and pulled out the Rudy O'Bannion case file from what seemed like a lifetime ago.

It didn't take long to understand why it seemed to have no importance when Ursula and I researched my cases. There wasn't much there, and what was there was routine and incomplete. Ursula wouldn't have known how incomplete it was, but looking at it with a new perspective, I saw it all too clearly.

There was an easy explanation—it was the last case before my crack-up. I killed an innocent man, spent time in a mental hospital, struggled with recovery, avoided prosecution, and finally moved to Mexico to escape from it all.

With all that going on, my record of the O'Bannion case piffled into nothing, along with my memory of most of it.

Some of it came back to me while I shuffled through the file and took a closer look. Rudy O'Bannion was a punk drug dealer who operated out of a small town in Northern California, not far from Lake Tahoe. He mostly dealt in opioids, drugs that blew through the country like a plague, addicting what sometimes seemed like entire populations, often in small-town America. Much of the news reportage, and the movie and TV versions that always followed such a juicy story, concentrated on the evils of Big Pharma and its bloodthirsty quest for bigger profits.

O'Bannion and creatures like him worked in the cracks, taking advantage of desperate people who were already enslaved to opioids but didn't have ready access to bent doctors and pharmacists for a steady supply.

How they got hooked didn't matter. They needed what they needed, and they needed it now and for the rest of their lives if they didn't get help. O'Bannion, who was only twenty-five, happily supplied it for as long as they could pay his outrageous price. When they couldn't, he dumped them and moved on to other victims.

The opioids O'Bannion peddled were brought into the country across the Canadian and Mexican borders, and in no way did they conform to Federal Drug Administration standards, which made what he was doing even more dangerous. There could have been anything in the junk he peddled.

My investigation was on the far periphery of the bigger case, which is often the way of the private investigator. I didn't even know there *was* a bigger case until I started looking.

I was employed by a Santa Barbara, California, architect whose ski-instructor sister lived near one of the resorts in the Sierra Nevada mountains of Northern California. She blew out her knee on the job. As an independent contractor, if she didn't work, she didn't get paid. Thanks to what she did for a living, her medical insurance was expensive and minimal because, as an independent contractor, she had to pay for it herself.

She tried to come back too soon and resorted to opioids to deal with the pain. When she got hooked and fell into the clutches of Rudy O'Bannion, the bottom fell out of her life. She lost everything, including her job, her home, and a longtime relationship.

My client didn't know anything about it until he found out that his sister was living on the street. He brought her to his home in Santa Barbara and employed me to find out how it happened, who was responsible, and how he could have that person drawn and quartered. He promised that, whatever it took, he and his sister would work together to end her addiction and get her life back.

I saw right away that O'Bannion didn't bother to cover his tracks very well. Several jurisdictions of law enforcement were already deep into my case, and several others with O'Bannion at the center.

The rest was so easy that Inspector Clouseau could have handled it.

Once my investigation finished, I gave a deposition and, with my client's approval, turned over all the evidence I had accumulated. With so much other evidence already in hand, I wasn't required to testify at the trial, though I did show up in the courtroom, and my name was mentioned. It was pretty simple all around.

The information I provided made a nice addition to the pile, but it certainly wasn't necessary to get a conviction.

And that was fine with me. I was paid to service my client, not the law. Judging by the limited contents of my case file, it appeared that I did my job well, or at least well enough, even if I didn't remember most of it and didn't follow through the way I normally would.

Rudy O'Bannion was found guilty after a short jury trial. Presumably, he went to prison, but I didn't have that in the file. If he did go to prison, I didn't know where.

Sloppy work, Cruickshank.

For all I knew, his lawyers latched onto some technicality and the conviction was overturned on appeal, or he escaped and was working on his tan somewhere in the South Pacific.

My client paid me in good time and said that he planned to take a leave from his business to tend to his sister. He trusted his employees to carry on without him for a while. I didn't know how all that turned out either.

That was it, except for a trial transcript. I didn't remember asking or paying for a transcript, or who provided it. The transcript wasn't signed and had no obvious official certification, another omission on my part. I had no way of knowing how accurate it might be, though it more than likely did well enough with the big picture.

According to the transcript, O'Bannion was sentenced to three years in prison with the likelihood of five years' probation upon release. There was nothing about what happened after the trial, such as an appeal, nor did I expect to find such things in a transcript. Getting such information to round out the file was my responsibility, and I blew it.

Given the extent of O'Bannion's guilt, the relatively

light sentence was surprising, even for a first-time offender. He must have had good, and no doubt expensive, lawyers.

The punk's cockiness came through loud and clear in the transcript, which probably did him no favors when it came to sentencing. I knew the type. His family or someone he knew well probably had influence, which he assumed would protect him, though the transcript didn't address that. Again, there was no reason why it would.

The more I read, the more I got the sense of a young man who was too inexperienced and probably too dumb to be so sure of himself but didn't know it. He should have played it humble and contrite on the stand, but the twit couldn't bring himself to do it. With the spotlight on him, he did everything but strut. A kid who was always coddled and protected, he had no sense of consequences because there had never been any. Until the moment the judge announced his sentence, he assumed that he'd get off because he always did.

If O'Bannion went to prison and didn't get into trouble inside, chances are he got out early, say after two or two-and-a-half years. If so, he'd still be on probation if he got the full five years. A probation officer somewhere could tell me his current location. If that didn't work, I'd find another way. There was always another way.

That was it.

I pulled up a legal pad and started writing questions that the incomplete file did not address. As often happened, it started a chain, with one thought leading to the next until the list of questions was longer, and more discouraging, than I expected.

Where was Rudy O'Bannion?

What was he up to these days?

Who did all that coddling and protecting? His family? A mentor?

What about his family? Who were they, and where did they get the clout I assumed they had? Money? Power? Influence? All the above?

Where did O'Bannion get the money and make the contacts to get into the opioids business in the first place? It's not the kind of expense you can throw on a Visa card or a contact you'll make down at the Moose Lodge.

Did the answer to that question come back to family?

If so, was the family in on it, too, and Rudy just the front man? Or was he working on his own, which brought me back to the mentor possibility?

I was reminded of what the assassin said about his feeling that his client was experienced in the dark side, and perhaps even a bad character of some kind himself, though not a high-ranking or smart one, much like the instigator of my attempted murder.

But the assassin's estimate of upper middle age or even older didn't fit Rudy O'Bannion.

Hmm.

I tried a deeper look online, but couldn't find anything else. That was one of the problems with the disappearance of newspapers, especially medium and small-town newspapers. A lot of stuff happens that's never reported or recorded anywhere. Stories end before they're fully told, if they're told at all.

And where there is no light, bad things happen.

CHAPTER 23

THE LOS ANGELES PD detective lieutenant I contacted when I was throwing out lines to catch information was the first to call back to say he had something. I called him. And he called me. We played phone tag for most of the day before finally connecting.

His name was Andy Barcelo, a happily married man with two teenage kids, a son and a daughter. Retirement was about ten years away. He was the kind of reliable hand that every good law enforcement organization needs, no matter if it's the FBI or a three-member police department in Mayberry—a walking, talking version of a Swiss army knife. If you want something done right, no matter what it is, get Barcelo.

"I got a contact for you," he said. "I've got some information, too, though you probably won't like it."

"Let's start with the information I won't like and get it over with," I said.

"Rudy O'Bannion is dead. He didn't last long inside. You didn't say so, but I assume you knew that he went to prison. He killed himself after six months."

I didn't expect that one. By the time O'Bannion killed himself, we'd moved to Cabo, so it's no surprise that I didn't hear about it. In those days, I wasn't paying attention.

But why would the assassin give me the name of a dead man? It was another addition to my growing list of questions.

"What happened?"

"O'Bannion was a good-looking young guy who quickly found out that he wasn't nearly as tough as he thought he was. Almost from his first day inside, he made a lot of new friends, if you know what I mean. You can imagine the rest."

"I'm afraid I can," I said. "How did he do it?"

"He managed to hang himself with his own clothes. I don't have the details, though I can get them if you think they're pertinent. But there's no doubt it was suicide. Anybody who really wants to will find a way, you know that. Put yourself in his place—abused and terrified every minute. Knowing that for the first time in your life, you have no protection and faced at least two more years of it even if you got out early.

"Anyway, that's the official unofficial line, and it sounds right to me," Barcelo concluded. "It does happen."

"Yeah, it does," I agreed. "Who's the contact?"

"A guy named Santiago Baca, though everybody calls him Jim. He was with the Sheriff's Department during the investigation that put O'Bannion in prison, one of a lotta guys from the feds to local who worked the case, including you, which I didn't know until I started looking."

"I was way outside the main investigation," I explained. "Working the case hardly describes it. What I did didn't mean much except to my client, which was all I cared about. I did turn over what I found, with my client's okay, but they didn't need it to put O'Bannion away."

"Sounds like it means something to somebody now, or you wouldn't be asking," he said.

Barcelo had just given me a chance to explain what I was up to. When I let it pass, he continued with the story.

"Anyway, sometime after the O'Bannion case, Baca made captain. Then he ran for sheriff and didn't get it. Instead of playing out his string until retirement, he said to hell with it and walked away early. The people I talked to say he was by far the better candidate and the department's rank and file were rooting for him. But voters went for an empty suit with an expensive haircut who made a lot of promises and now makes a fool out of himself on a monthly basis.

"Baca and his wife still live in Northern California, only now it's somewhere between Placerville and Lake Tahoe. They have a boutique wine business in the foothills. There are a lot of 'em up there. He grows his own grapes, buys from other growers to supplement what he grows, and hires help when he needs it to harvest, do the bottling, the whole shot. He says that he doesn't make much money at it. He and his wife just like doing it."

"Kind of a hobby," I said.

"I guess, though that's a helluva hard hobby. I think I'd rather take up golf, and I don't even like golf."

"He'll talk to me?" I asked.

"Yeah...well, maybe. Here's the rub: He'll only do it face-to-face. He wants to get a read on you first. He knows *about* you, with all the celebrity crap a while back. That's the problem.

"He asked me not to tell you this, but I will anyway so you'll be ready. He wants to make sure you're not a spot-light-hunting jerk trying to get on some stupid TV show or something for another round of fame. He said, and I'm quoting, 'I want to be sure this guy has real purpose.'

"I told him you're okay and didn't ask for any of that other stuff to happen. I even gave him a couple of contacts to ask about you, including Eddie Heenan. I hope that's okay?"

When I assured him that it was, Barcelo continued, "Baca believes me, I think, but he still wants to see you for himself. He won't jerk you around. If he decides not to talk, you'll know it from the get-go."

"So I'm supposed to go up there, wherever it is?"

"Yeah, it looks like it, unless he falls in love with you over the phone, or something."

"And he's worth it?"

"I guess it depends on how bad you want what you're after. But yeah, I think he is. He's the best source I could find. You know it's almost always better in person anyway. Baca's a straight shooter who knows a lot of inside stuff. If he does talk, you'll get the story, and maybe some good leads out of it if that's what you're looking for."

"Okay, I get it," I said. "Baca sounds okay to me, too, I guess."

"Good," Barcelo said. "I'll give you his number and he'll give you his address when you call and set up a meeting."

"One more thing," I said. "Do you know who claimed O'Bannion's body, or who was next of kin?"

"I have no idea. That's way out of my territory. But I'm sure Baca either knows or can find out pretty easy."

A trip to the Northern California boondocks was a pain in the ass but I had to do it.

I made the call.

CHAPTER 24

WHICH IS how I found myself driving along the picturesque roads of the Sierra Nevada foothills in Northern California between Sacramento and Lake Tahoe. Gold country of yesterday turned into wine country today.

Getting there was simple, if time-consuming. After a ridiculously early start, I flew to Los Angeles, a flight I mostly slept through. I waited. Changed aircraft. Flew to Sacramento. Rented a baby poop green SUV at the airport and, with GPS guiding me, found Highway 50 and drove east almost to the Sierra Nevada Mountain range, which loomed mighty in the distance surrounding Lake Tahoe.

In my brief research to figure out where the hell I was going and what I'd find when I got there, I discovered that there are a lot of wineries in the area that make up the Sierra foothills wine region—basically El Dorado, Amador, and Calaveras counties. My search did not reveal any jumping frogs. It was the first time Mark Twain ever let me down.

The foothills wineries are not as popular as their Napa Valley brethren to the west, bigger and better known operations roughly northwest of Sacramento, about halfway to the Pacific coast. Drawing from the large population of the San Francisco Bay Area, they are well-positioned to get thousands of tourists every day. On weekends, the traffic can be almost bumper to bumper from one winery to the next. Even though I just got here, I found the foothills setting less commercial, not so crowded, and more attractive.

Every so often, along the rolling hills and winding roads, I saw a sign pointing down some back road to a little, and sometimes not so little, winery. Most of them were open for tasting and, more important to the winemakers, for buying and shipping. As the GPS faded in and out thanks to the towering trees and rolling countryside that sometimes blocked the signal, I went old-school by relying on signage, a map, and Baca's directions.

I was looking for a sign leading to the E&S Winery. When I called Baca to set up our meeting, he explained that the E was for his wife, Eleanor, and the S for himself, Santiago. Just as I began to think I'd missed it, a modest sign with black letters on a white background appeared on a white wooden post with an arrow pointing to the right down a narrow two-lane road.

I followed the tree-lined road for almost a mile, then, obedient to another sign, turned left down a dirt road where I raised a mighty cloud of dust and found the winery about a quarter of a mile later in a nice little glen, though it might have been a glade, or even a meadow. I never knew the difference.

The E&S Winery was not on a well-traveled road where you'd run into it by accident and stop on impulse. You had to look for it. You had to want to go there. I figured E&S wines must have a good reputation to draw anyone to such an out-of-the-way location.

I pulled into a gravel parking lot big enough to hold a dozen cars. The parking boundaries were set by railroad ties laid out in front of a tasting room and shop that was done in an alpine style that might have inspired yodeling. There was a second floor that I figured must be the living quarters.

A big two-story unpainted cider-block building in the back housed the storage and wine-making apparatus. At least that was my guess. For all I knew about wine making, it could have been a home for abandoned elephants.

I parked next to a white BMW convertible with the top down. This being a weekday, it was the only other car in the lot. As I got out of the dust-covered rental, stretched and worked the kinks out of my back and legs, Dave Brubeck played *Take Five* on my phone. It was Ursula, probably with information about Burnside.

I texted that I'd call her later. I wanted to finish, or at least start, my business with Baca.

I'd come a long way, and it was time to catch a break.

I was overdue.

Of course, I always thought I was overdue.

CHAPTER 25

I WAITED my turn at the counter alongside a young couple who belonged to the BMW. His brown suede shoes had gold buckles and his feet had no socks. His sunglasses were fetchingly backward, like he had eyes in the back of his head. She was very blonde, and nicely tanned and toned to go with it, with mid-thigh white shorts to show off the tanning and the toning. They were thoughtfully sampling tiny sips of wine and carefully swishing it around like it might be the first step on the way to world peace.

I gave my business card to the even younger man with a ponytail who supervised the tasting. His eyebrows rose a bit when he saw that I was a private investigator.

I explained that Baca was expecting me. He left the couple to their orgasmic wine experience and opened a door behind the counter.

I heard him say, "Dad, a private detective named Ethan Cruickshank is here to see you," before returning to his post, where he watched me out of the corner of his eye.

After the reasonable amount of time it might take to

wrap up whatever he was doing, Baca emerged from the back room.

He was not a tall man, five or six inches under my six two, but gave the appearance of being even shorter because the rest of him was so massive that he looked almost square.

At one point in his life, Baca must have been a serious power lifter. His shoulders were nearly as wide as the doorway, and his upper body seemed on the verge of bursting free of his black t-shirt like the transformation of the Incredible Hulk. His khaki shorts, battered hiking boots, and white socks showed that he didn't neglect his legs in his workouts, unlike many men who concentrate only on the show muscles so they can flex well.

Even at his age—early sixties, according to Barcelo, the LAPD detective—Baca looked like he could toss around wine barrels like Nerf balls. He was just a little soft around the middle, perhaps an indicator that he didn't have as much time for regular workouts as he once did, or maybe he gave it up as a result of injury or bore-dom. He was mostly bald, with a fringe of white hair that he didn't bother to shave like some do to show that they may be bald, but it's on purpose. Really.

He reached a beefy arm across the counter. "Hi, I'm Jim Baca." The rough calluses on his hand indicated that he did a lot of the labor around the winery himself. The handshake was firm, but no bone-crusher.

"C'mon around," he said, waving me around the end of the counter. "It's a nice day. We can sit outside unless you'd rather not."

I'd been cooped up in airports, airplanes, and cars most of the day, so sitting outside in the Sierra foothills on a blue-sky California afternoon was okay with me.

We passed through his messy office in the back of the tasting room and settled facing each other at a redwood picnic table in a large grassy area to one side of the alpine building. A few other tables and benches were haphazardly scattered around, along with a half dozen white Adirondack chairs.

The feeling between us was more tentative than friendly, though not at all hostile. We were testing each other. Despite thinking about it during the flight, I still wasn't sure about the best way to get started, and he still wasn't sure he wanted to hear it.

I noticed that Baca had an old-fashioned yellow number two pencil with a nice sharp point settled at the top of his right ear. I hadn't seen that look in a long time, and for some reason, it relaxed me. It was like comfort food for the eyes.

"We get a lotta people who drive up here, buy our wine, and have a little picnic," he explained, waving his hand at the picture-postcard surroundings.

"Wine being what it is, that's often followed by a nap. When they wake up, they usually buy more wine to take home. We'd like to put in a little take-out restaurant for people who don't bring their own food and decide to picnic at the last minute, just sandwiches, fried chicken, and stuff like that, but we're not quite there yet. The longer we can keep people here, the more they're likely to buy. We do pretty well selling to restaurants, too, though we're not in grocery stores or wine shops. We don't produce that kind of volume, and it'll be a while before we do, if ever. I'm not really sure I want to get that big. A boutique winery is fine with me."

"I can see the appeal of a little afternoon snooze out here," I said, taking in the peaceful setting. "I might be tempted to curl up under a tree myself. Since he called you Dad, I assume the young man inside is your son."

"Geez, you must be a detective." Baca grinned to show he was joking, not mocking. "Yeah, Davy's going to

Stanford. He helps Eleanor and me when he's on break, or when he can get away for a long weekend. He says he wants to be a lawyer. Since he's my son, I try not to hold it against him. There's always a chance he'll change his mind. Then again, maybe the my-son-the-lawyer thing wouldn't be so bad. Like they say, it's only ninety-nine percent of the lawyers that give the rest a bad name.

"You know anything about wine?" he asked.

"I know what I like, what I don't like, and why I like or don't like it," I said.

"As a consumer, that's pretty much all you need," he said. "A lot of the places around here specialize in Zinfandel. There's also some really good Petite Syrah and excellent blends, too. What we have going for us in this area of the foothills is a combination of altitude, we're at about 2,500 feet, and a lot of granite in the soil. With all the granite, the vines have to work hard, which makes them stronger. Deep, healthy vines lead to a more finished wine.

"Even when it gets hot in the day, most of the time it cools down as much as twenty-five or thirty degrees at night, which helps the grapes retain the acidity needed for balance. Unlike down in the central valley, where they're in a serious drought more often than not, we usually get enough rain, or runoff from the snowmelt in the Sierra, though not always."

There was more coming, and I was trying to pay attention, but Baca caught me at it.

"Sorry," he said, shaking his head to emphasize the apology. "I've been doing this for a few years now, mostly working seven days a week, and I'm still as enthusiastic as I was on the first day. It doesn't even seem like work to me. Sometimes I forget that not everybody feels that way. If Ellie were here, she'd poke me in the ribs with a sharp elbow and tell me to shut up before you passed out from boredom. I know you didn't come here to talk about wine."

"No, but it's interesting," I lied.

"I appreciate you at least pretending," he said.

We both laughed. The tentative mood had shifted so that now we felt at ease with each other.

"So tell me what you're doing and what brought you here. I know what Barcelo told me, though he didn't know everything, or maybe he didn't tell me everything he knew. At his suggestion, I talked to your pal Eddie Heenan, who thinks you walk on water. But I'd like to hear the story from you.

"By the way," he added. "Heenan was a little put out that you didn't call him so he could hook up with you at the LA airport or meet you here. What is he, your body-guard, or something?"

"Just a friend," I said. "A good one."

"Sounds like it," Baca said. "I know Heenan by repu-tation. A friend like that can come in handy."

I was surprised to hear what Heenan said about me until I realized that I would say pretty much the same thing about him.

And so I started talking.

CHAPTER 26

I DIDN'T HOLD MUCH BACK.

I named names and dates going back to before our move to Cabo and the reasons for the move. I was tired of withholding information from people I liked in order to protect people I did not know and who might not deserve it anyway. I felt like reticence was getting in my way.

I did keep quiet about a few things, though not many. If that made me a liar and a hypocrite, I could live with it. I've been called worse. My need for information overrode everything else.

I also hoped that if Baca believed that I was being straight with him, it might open the information floodgate.

The tale took a while, mostly because I also told him what I didn't know and needed to find out.

When I finished, Baca took a moment to think it over, a serious and methodical man who did and said nothing of importance without due consideration. He was comfortable with silence, too. I didn't mind the silence either. It meant that I gave him something to chew on. It was a good sign that he didn't tell me to get lost.

"That is one helluva story," he said. "I appreciate your telling it to a stranger like me. I doubt that it was easy. While you talked, I remembered seeing your name in the Rudy O'Bannion thing. I knew it was there, but now I remember the context."

"I'm surprised you made the connection because I wasn't that involved," I said. "Like I told Barcelo, I was just servicing my client and tried to keep away from the other stuff as much as possible.

"You know how that goes. Do your own thing and try not to call attention to yourself so you don't get big-footed by the state guys, the FBI, or whoever else might be involved. They almost always want you to shut down what you're doing because they think you'll blunder around and mess up their case. At least, that's what they claim. Most of the time, it's more of a turf thing."

"The O'Bannions, father and son, thought you were pretty damn involved," Baca said. "Maybe you didn't know that?"

When I shook my head to indicate that I didn't, Baca explained what he meant.

"Right or wrong, the father pinned a lot of what happened to Rudy on you. It was easier for him to blame the one guy who showed up and started sniffing around not long before his son was arrested, went to prison, and killed himself than blame half the law enforcement in this part of the state, or, more properly, blame the kid.

"At the department, we saw that kind of thinking many times. When bad things happen, it has to be some-body's fault, and it sure as hell can't be their little darling, or wife, husband, best friend, or whatever. An institution is too big to blame, much less try to do anything about it, but an individual is easy. We didn't think anything would come of it because, as far as we knew, nothing ever did.

There's just a lot of huffing and puffing, and then it goes away."

Baca looked off into the middle distance, working his way through the memories.

"We should have warned you, I guess, but in the craziness of everyday work, it didn't seem to amount to much and just kind of got lost. What happened was the kid's own fault, of course, but his father wasn't about to accept that. He needed a target for his anger, and you were it. For most of us, you were just a name in a report."

"I had no idea," I admitted. "I didn't keep up with it afterward. I should have."

I knew that Danny O'Bannion was Rudy's father, and that's basically all I knew about him.

"From what you just said, you had a lot going on." Baca rose to his feet. "After all that, even though you did most of the talking, I need a glass of wine. Want some?"

"Sure," I said. "Whatever you recommend. I don't like sweet wines, though."

"Good," he said. "I don't either."

Baca went back through his office to the tasting room and returned shortly with two wine glasses, a pitcher of ice water, two glasses for the water, and a bottle of wine, all of it balanced on a tray. As he opened the wine without bothering to set it on the redwood table, his big hands made the bottle look half the size.

Pouring the wine, he said, "I think this will do very nicely. If it doesn't, we're screwed. It's the best we've got."

It was just fine.

So was the second glass.

CHAPTER 27

"I GUESS the first thing you should know is that the old man was a genius."

"The old man?" I asked.

"Rudy's grandfather, Danny O'Bannion," replied Baca. "The guy who started it all. He set up the machinery that's still running after all these years despite the best efforts of his chicken-shit son and his even dumber grandson to screw it up."

I shook my head again to show that I wasn't up to speed.

"I thought Danny O'Bannion was Rudy's father, and I have no idea what machinery you're talking about."

Baca smiled. "Yeah, maybe I am getting a little ahead of myself. The story goes back a long way, and it's been part of my life since I joined the department."

"Assume I don't know anything and start at the beginning, wherever that is," I said.

"I can do that," Baca said, taking a fortifying sip of wine. "Some of what I'll tell you is fact, some of it is supposition that's almost certainly true, and some of it is my own opinion. I'll explain what I mean as I go along.

"The original Danny O'Bannon came out here in the

fifties, a few years before the nineteen sixty Winter Olympics in Squaw Valley that pretty much put Tahoe and surroundings on the map. Some casinos and resorts were already there, of course, but the place wasn't internationally, or even nationally, known yet, nothing like Vegas.

"Underneath the usual legitimate cover, most of the casinos were mobbed up to some degree. The best-known probably was Cal-Neva, right on the border of California and Nevada. It even had a white line running down the middle of the main room. One side was California, the other Nevada. Frank Sinatra was a major owner. Sinatra's buddy, Sam Giancana, the Chicago mobster, was what they used to call a silent partner.

"In those days, everybody was looking for the next Las Vegas. Combine Tahoe with Reno, which is only about twenty miles away and has casinos and resorts of its own, and it looked like it could happen there. For a variety of reasons, it never quite did. Vegas still gets most of the attention. For one thing, it's easier to get to and a lot closer to all those millions of poor bastards who live in LA. But Tahoe still got pretty big time, no matter how you look at it.

"O'Bannion was smart, and Tahoe being kind of under the radar worked in his favor. He had connections where he came from back east and used them wisely. He kept his profile low and was careful never to be seen as too aggressive while usually getting what he wanted and not making a big deal out of it when he didn't. That kind of reasonableness attracted people because they knew they could do business with him. He made himself so useful to the top guys that he became indispensable. In his quietly efficient way, he became a top guy, too.

"In several operations, O'Bannion eased into small ownership positions, but once again, he wasn't greedy about it. If one of the big guys owned twenty-five or thirty percent, O'Bannion might have five or ten percent, acquired legitimately because he had no criminal record and the state had no reason to keep him out.

"He also provided or controlled services like private gambling by the very highest rollers, prostitutes, alcohol, and some drugs, though he always seemed a leery of that stuff 'cause there's more violence attached. Makes it too unpredictable and harder to keep everything in line. Too messy for him, I guess. Control was always very important to Danny O'Bannion.

"Over time, in addition to everything else, he developed a kind of side specialty: Solving tricky personal and business problems for high rollers, celebrities, and even other casino owners, though he was a lot more than just a simple fixer.

"O'Bannion had remarkable instincts. He could anticipate a problem before anybody else and saw the law of unintended consequences in a way no one else did. Even when he didn't own a piece of a casino, he was well paid for his services. You name it, and O'Bannion took care of it, or knew somebody who could, and he did it quietly and efficiently. He knew where all the bodies were buried and, like they say, information is power.

"But I think the main reason for his long run is that he kept out of the public eye. Even some insiders didn't know the scope of everything he did. When other guys got in trouble with the feds, or were done in by their own associates like Giancana, gunned down in his own kitchen, or Johnny Roselli, stuffed alive into a steel drum that was found in the water near Miami, O'Bannion was careful to keep his nose clean. He never lost his independence and managed to stay neutral no matter how much the other guys pissed on each other. Doing what he did, and considering the sharks he did it with, that's no small accomplishment. I mean, I really can't think of anybody else who pulled it off."

Baca said that O'Bannion married an ambitious show-girl from Oklahoma named Ruthie Koslow. Their son, born six months later, was an only child they named Danny Junior, who everybody called Dan-Dan, even after he grew up, went to work for his father, and took over the operation when the old man died at his desk after a stroke.

"He *hates* being called Dan-Dan," Baca said. "He always did. It makes him sound like a little kid. He was constantly compared to his father anyway, and the stupid nickname only made it worse. The result is that he spent his life doing what the shrinks call over-compensating, at least that's my take. He comes off like a tough guy, but if you're around him long enough, it just makes him seem a little silly. Where his father was the coolest customer you'd ever meet, Dan-Dan runs hot all the time and doesn't have the chops to back it up.

"Ruthie, Danny's wife and Dan-Dan's mother, knew exactly what she was getting into when she married Danny. It turned out that she was a natural. They had their ups and downs like anybody else, but Ruthie and Danny worked alongside each other until the day he died. A lot of people thought that she might be even be smarter than he was, not to mention being the family hard ass who wasn't afraid of anybody. But nobody could beat his instincts, or the smooth way he could work people without them knowing it. I've always believed that she played a bigger role in the empire they built than anybody suspected. However it worked, they were a hell of a team for a long time.

"Dan-Dan never lived up to what his parents hoped that he would be. He knew it, they knew it, and he knew they knew it. He felt the pressure of their disappointment every day.

"Like I said, he still tries to make up for it with tough-guy bullshit like he's watched *The Godfather* or *Goodfellas* a hundred and fifty times, but after about five minutes he never fools anybody who really knows him.

"Even if you cut him some slack, and most people do out of respect for his parents, the real problem is that he's not that bright. And his kid, Rudy, was even dumber than Daddy, and an arrogant little prick at the same time, a classic example of somebody born on third base who thinks they hit a triple. The gene pool got real shallow from one generation to the next, if you know what I mean.

"As far as anybody knew, the opioid operation was strictly Rudy's idea and his to run, which guaranteed that it would eventually fail with a great big thud. For one thing, he couldn't keep from calling attention to himself and drove around doing business in some kind of expensive bright red Italian flash car, one of those things that looks like it's going a hundred miles an hour even when it's standing still.

"The kid was a stupid cliché from head to toe. He wasn't ready for the big time and never would be. Everybody knows that he got the money to get started from his father. I mean, who else would give it to him? Dan-Dan knew that his son was a doofus, but couldn't bring himself to say no to anything he wanted, even when he knew that he should for the kid's own good. He posed like a father, the same way he posed like a tough guy."

"Sometimes you use the present tense when you mention…Dan-Dan." I felt silly even saying the name. "Is he still around?"

"Yeah, Dan-Dan still runs what's left, though he's getting on. He's one of those guys who seems even older than his years, like he's got a lot of city miles on him. The O'Bannion clout isn't close to what it used to be, but the family is fantastically wealthy. They made a hell of a lot of money over the years and managed to keep most of it through the usual slick accounting. I wouldn't be surprised if they still have a percentage of the casino action.

"I'm sure Rudy was gonna take over the operation at some point, which would have wrecked everything like hitting a brick wall. Now I don't know what's gonna happen once Dan-Dan goes. There's nobody left. Probably there'll be some fighting while the younger guys from outside pick at the bones."

"Who claimed the kid's body?" I asked.

"I'm sure Dan-Dan did, or more likely had somebody do it for him. Word was they had it cremated."

"So there was no third party involved in all this?" I asked. "It was all family? There was no outside mentor, or anything?"

When Baca replied with a simple "no chance," I asked another question, one that just occurred to me.

"What about the mother?" I asked. "What was her name? Ruthie? If Dan-Dan is so dumb, maybe he relies on her, or at least did until she died, and that's really what kept the operation running for so long, even if you make it sound like it's on life support these days."

"That's an interesting thought, something I've considered myself," Baca said. "The thing is, nobody knows. There's no record of Ruthie's death. Actually, there's no record of her at all for twenty years or more. As far as I know, nobody has seen or heard from her for at least that long. If she's still alive, she's older than dirt and never goes anywhere, at least not that anybody knows. Most people think she's dead, and there's no reason to think she's not. But I'm not so sure, though I don't have fact one to base that on. It's kinda hard to imagine her doing a Howard Hughes looney turn if she's still alive, but what the hell, it happened to Howard Hughes.

"Anyway, there we are," he concluded. "Dan-Dan is getting old, dumb as ever, and his son and heir is dead. The contacts and associations that gave the family business meaning and protection over the years are dying out. It's a different world now. The O'Bannions are a relic. Their time has passed, and there isn't a soul on either side of the law who would mind if Dan-Dan dropped dead or got killed and the world moved on from all the disruption he causes. And I think he senses that, even if he probably couldn't articulate it.

"After Rudy's death, I got the feeling that he was lashing out, part from long-simmering frustration and part from desperation. His already bad temper got even worse. One of his targets—and maybe the only serious target—was you, and he can't let it go.

"I don't know if Dan-Dan ever really loved Rudy. I kind of doubt it. I don't think he was capable. But it was important that he seemed to because that's what a man does. It's written in the Manly Code of Crapola, or something. When Rudy was sent to prison and killed himself, his father had to do something. He couldn't just let it pass because it would make him look weak. The irony is that everybody knows he's weak."

"That still doesn't explain the different style hits," I said. "One was smart, expensive, and professional. The other was stupid, cheap, and badly done."

"Yeah," Baca agreed, taking a last sip of wine that finished off the bottle. "The first one was how Danny or Ruthie would have handled it. Don't use anybody close that could be tied to you. Spend what it takes to get the best. Be patient so that it's done right, with virtually no chance of blowback. If the assassin guy hadn't collapsed in the desert after shooting Goldstein, nobody would have known a thing. But the second one against you... geez, I dunno."

"From what you say, maybe it's not that hard to figure," I said. "Don't take this wrong, but like you said, this stuff has been part of your life for a long time. Maybe you need to step back a little."

I felt a rising eagerness that almost made me squirm on the bench, like I had tumbled onto treasure I didn't expect to find. I leaned forward, with my forearms on the redwood table, and took a deep breath before taking the plunge.

"The man who killed Dina used some of the same words to describe the guy who hired him that you did describing Dan-Dan," I said. "The words 'stupid' and 'Dan-Dan' do seem to go together, but that sounds like the second hit.

"Tell me," I asked, "does Dan-Dan smoke?"

The out-of-left-field question showed up all over Baca's face.

"Yeah, he does," he said.

"Does he have a smoker's cough?"

"Same answer," Baca said. "Pretty bad, too. It beats the hell out of him sometimes."

"He's the guy, for sure," I said. "There's too much coincidence, otherwise. He fits the assassin's description exactly."

"But that first hit, it's just not Dan-Dan," Baca protested. "For one thing, he's way too cheap. No matter how much he wanted it done, he'd never spend that kind of money. What did you say, something over a million?"

"Probably closer to two," I said. "To answer that question, I give you two words: Mommie Dearest."

"Holy Jesus!" Baca's eyes widened as he picked up on

my feeling of revelation. "You think Ruthie's still alive and she's the one who pulled the strings!"

"If anything about this whole mess makes sense, that does," I said. "I think the first time was all hers, and he followed her instructions like a good boy, apparently the way he always did.

"She told him how to find this particular guy, a man who never fails. She told him what to say and how to say it, almost like a ventriloquist. The assassin said that the guy he talked to didn't seem surprised or even care when he was told how much the job cost. I think the reason is that his mother already spelled it out for him, how he'd have to suck it up and spend the money. The times they talked, or communicated in other ways, she was probably right there. He said the conversations were weird, like something else was going on at the same time. I bet she was giving Dan-Dan instructions, even if they weren't verbal, and he was constantly checking with her.

"But the attempt on me was all his. As time passed, he still had the itch to make a move against me and finally decided to do something about it. If Ruthie is still alive, has all her marbles, and is as smart as you say, she didn't know what he was up to, or she would have made him call it off, or at least do it right.

"Or maybe she died sometime after Dina's murder and before the attempt on me, so she was no longer around to control her son? Or did he do it to defy her? A big up-yours to good old Mom, who was disappointed by him all his life, something she probably made pretty clear, if what you say is on the mark. If she's dead now, well, that explains it, too. He did it on his own and did it badly.

"I know that a lot of this is getting into psychology, and maybe I don't know what I'm talking about. But I've spent a lot of time with shrinks of all kinds, so maybe I do."

Baca sat back on the bench and blew out a lungful of air as he considered what I said.

"Okay, let's say you're right, and it sounds pretty good to me as a working theory," he said. "What are you gonna do about it? What *can* you do about it?"

"Baca, you've been a big help, and I really appreciate it, but I don't think you want to hear the answer to that question. Hell, I'm not even sure I have an answer yet. But, well…"

Baca gave me a long, thoughtful look.

"No," he said. "I didn't hear a thing."

CHAPTER 28

AFTER MORE REFLECTION, Baca said, "Yep, it's better that I didn't hear that last thing."

"What last thing?" I said.

"That's what I mean," he said. "You get older, maybe you start hearing voices."

I didn't know it in any way I could prove, but every instinct I had told me that Dan-Dan and his aged ex-showgirl mother, Ruthie, conspired to murder my wife, Dina, by hiring the best, an assassin who never failed.

Then, years later, dumbo Dan-Dan tried to kill me using a cheap local meathead. Maybe his mother was still alive and maybe she wasn't, but if she was as smart as she was supposed to be, she never would have approved it.

I knew that Baca agreed, though he didn't say so because he couldn't, suspecting what I might do next and refusing to hear it. Once a cop, always a cop. To his credit, there was a line that he could not, or would not, cross.

We had talked enough. It had already been a long day and I needed time alone to think. In the midst of all these healthy grapes and excellent wine, I needed a beer, too. Maybe more than one. And I was hungry.

I stood up and Baca followed.

"How long you gonna be around?" he asked.

"I don't know. I'm reserved at a bed-and-breakfast in Sonora. They said business is slow enough so that I can keep the room for a while if I need it."

"I have an idea," Baca said. "I can clear my day tomorrow. Davy can cover for me. He'll probably like not having me looming around. Do you want to see where these characters live?"

I started a question and he quickly answered.

"Trust me, you're not gonna believe it. The place was started way back when the O'Bannions were at their peak and never really finished. There always seems to be something going on construction-wise. It may be the only flamboyant thing that Danny O'Bannion ever did, though it was really Ruthie's idea. Her husband's light never shined bright enough to satisfy her, even though that was his choice. She wanted the world to know. Around here, they call it the Castle, and you'll see why. Even if we just do a drive by and can't see that much from the road, you'll still get a sense of it."

"I would very much like to see it, if you don't mind taking the time," I said. "Like you said, just to get a sense of things. In a way I can't explain, sometimes stuff like that helps flesh things out."

"I know what you mean and it's no trouble at all," he said. "All this is making me feel like a cop again, except for that last part, the thing that I didn't hear because you never said it".

CHAPTER 29

WE AGREED to meet at eleven the next morning. I left the winery, drove to the bed-and-breakfast in Sonora, checked in, and dumped my roller bag in my room.

Like most such places, the room was too frilly for my taste, with too many cute little pillows that served no purpose, but the bed seemed comfortable and the decor wouldn't keep me awake at night.

I asked the cheerful owner if he could recommend a nearby restaurant. I explained that I was hungry, didn't require gourmet dining, and I'd be very happy if it served beer.

He directed me to a place a couple of miles away, one that was popular with the locals. As I wheeled into the restaurant's parking lot, it looked like it might rank somewhere between a Mom and Pop operation and a nice upscale restaurant. No lace tablecloths, but no greasy spoons either. That worked for me.

I parked and went inside. Once my eyes adjusted to the darker room, I saw that I was the only customer. It was too late for the lunch crowd and too early for dinner, but I hadn't eaten since a three a.m. breakfast of one hard-boiled egg, toast, and coffee, so I didn't care what time it was. At least the place was open.

An older gentleman with a scar across one cheek and the artificial dignity of a funeral director greeted me at the door and led me to a horseshoe-shaped booth done in red leather. I slid into one side of the booth and stayed there instead of moving to rear center so I wouldn't have to scoot along on my butt for what always seemed like a half mile before getting back to my feet, a decision that might have saved my life.

I really started liking the place when I saw they had Guinness on tap. I ordered one and told the creaky waiter wearing a white shirt and clip-on black bow tie to bring another one in about five minutes. After a long and infinitely satisfying drink, I began perusing the plastic-coated menu.

Which was when unexpected company dropped in.

He slid into the booth on the other side of the table. His face didn't register at first because my attention was drawn to the Glock in his right hand, which he set on the table sideways with his finger on the trigger and the weapon pointed at me.

"What the hell are you doing here, Cruickshank?" he said, his voice enriched by decades of alcohol and ciga-rettes. "You can't possibly be as dumb as walking in here makes you look."

"I was about to order dinner," I said. "I'm a big fan of lasagna, but the bolognese looks good, too. Then there's—"

"Shut the hell up!"

"That attitude won't enhance my review. You've lost a star already."

"I could shoot you right now and you couldn't do a thing to stop me. You are well and truly screwed."

He had me there. I wasn't armed. I couldn't take a

weapon on the flight, of course. Even if I somehow acquired one in wine country, I was wearing a polo shirt with jeans, desert boots, and no jacket. My new dinner companion could see that I had nothing to shoot back with if things took a bad turn, which they already had.

When in doubt, keep 'em talking, which is easier if they're cocky, know they have the advantage, and enjoy the hell out of it.

"I doubt that the management would appreciate early dinner arrivals being greeted by a dead body," I said.

"I am the management. Part owner, too. While you were making love to your beer, I had the "Closed for private party" sign put out and the door locked. Anybody who tries to come in will think we're getting ready for some special event tonight. We do 'em all the time. Once I shoot you, your body will be out the back door in about five minutes. Within an hour you'll be sinking to the bottom of Lake Tahoe with all the other assholes."

I believed him. The only thing I had going for me was that his eagerness to show off gave me a chance to size him up. He was a lot closer to older than Grandpa than younger than springtime. Confident though he was, he did not look like a man who possessed lightning reflexes. I sure hoped not.

I still had the plastic menu in my right hand. I laid it on the table and lowered my hand to my lap where he couldn't see it. I took a deep breath, shifted slightly, lowered my right shoulder a fraction, then raised it again. At the same time, I released my grip on the glass of Guinness with the other hand. I straightened up, then slumped and lowered my head like a beaten man.

At first, he didn't react to the small movements, though I knew he saw them. He probably thought I was squirming with fear, a reasonable assumption under the circumstances.

He finally had enough.

"Stop all the goddam wiggling," he demanded. "You're driving me nuts."

"Okay, but there is one thing you should know," I said.

"And what's that?"

"Not many people use ankle holsters these days. They're too hard to get to quickly. But being a traditional kind of guy, I just pulled a hideout from mine."

His eyes narrowed at the surprise turn in the conversation. I'd prepared him to believe me with all my little fidgets.

"It's pointed under the table right at your balls," I said. "It's only a little Beretta, and your manhood presents a tiny little target, I'm sure, but at this range, how can I miss?"

As I distracted him with phony threats, I snatched his Glock from the tabletop with my left hand. He was so enthralled by his power over me that he'd relaxed his grip, with his right hand lying on the weapon like a dead fish. I had the Glock on my side of the table before he realized that I'd reached for it. I was a lousy shot with my left hand, but we were so close it didn't matter.

"Okay, genius, now it's my turn to ask the questions. How do you know who I am?"

He licked his thin lips. He was nervous. Good.

"Everybody knows what you look like. The boss is obsessed with you. We've even got a picture of you around here someplace. He wants your head on a platter. It's been that way since what happened to Rudy. My people had you made the second you walked in. We couldn't believe the good luck. The guy at the door pressed a button that leads to a buzzer in my office upstairs, warning me to take a look. Besides, when I'm here, I make it a point to see everybody who comes in, if not right away, then soon as I can. We had you either way. You got some nerve comin' here."

Though he tried to keep up the act, his bravado had pretty much disappeared now that I had his weapon, but with it came a series of problems.

I thought them through as I made a motion like I was returning my Beretta to my ankle rig and switched the Glock to my right hand.

If I shot him, then what?

The old guy who showed me to the booth and the creaky waiter could ID me. Should I shoot them, too? Slaughtering old people was not a happy thought.

Was there more help around, either in the back, the kitchen, or upstairs?

It was early for dinner, but there had to be a cook and at least one or two more in the kitchen.

Was there any muscle around?

If there was, and they heard a shot, I couldn't get out of the restaurant without a fight. For all I knew, some goon was watching us right now, but didn't want to make a move with his boss in danger. All of which presented more unpleasant options.

Was all this being recorded on security cams, which would further identify me?

O'Bannion's people obviously knew who I was, but the local cops didn't know me from Farmer Brown. I wanted to keep it that way. If I got out of here, I wasn't sure about my next move, but I doubted that the local law would be inclined to help. I knew I could count on Baca, but I didn't want him to get involved that deeply.

I didn't see any cameras inside or out when I walked through the door, though these days, with miniature everything, that didn't mean much. But this place didn't look like it might house the last word in nano-technology, so I was probably safe there.

But probably is not certainty.

"You got a cell phone?" I asked.

He nodded, reluctantly.

"Hand it over. And be very careful. Two fingers only."

He did, with even more reluctance, using his thumb and index finger. It was a flip phone. A burner, no doubt.

"Here's what we're gonna do," I said. "You stand up. You turn around so your back is to me. I stand up. We walk to the door like we're joined at the hip. That thing that'll be poking in your side is your own Glock. Then we walk to my SUV out front. You get in the driver's side and crawl over to the passenger's seat so I don't have to worry about you running. I get in. I drive away. Way down the road someplace, I let you out. I keep the phone so you can't make any calls. By the time you get back here and call somebody for help, I'm long gone.

"If you don't do all of those things, if we are followed or interrupted in any way, I will shoot you with your own gun. It'll make a bigger, nastier hole than my Beretta, though your balls will be safe. The rest of you, not so much. Whatever happens to me after that won't do you much good, will it?"

It turned out that he was very good at following instructions.

CHAPTER 30

"YOU DID NOT TELL me that the bad guys own a restaurant a couple of miles from where I'm staying."

I let my passenger off just around the first bend in the road after we left the restaurant, about three-quarters of a mile away. He was glad to get away, but not happy to be on foot, and generally mad as hell. He probably hadn't walked anywhere in years.

I drove back to the bed-and-breakfast, noodling around on the way to make sure I wasn't followed, which would not be easy to do on country roads without much traffic. Guest parking was in front, but I parked in back so the rental couldn't be seen from the street. Nobody objected. I could have parked on the roof for all it mattered. The owners were just happy to have the business, though there was another rental parked out front, indicating that they had another customer.

I went up to my room and called Baca.

"I didn't know they owned a place like that," replied Baca. "The O'Bannions do have legitimate business interests, but I don't know all of 'em. Remember, I'm retired. I'm not in the loop anymore. Why is that important?"

"I hope my bed and breakfast isn't one of them," I said

"Don't worry, it's not. I know the owners. They're good people. What the hell happened?"

I explained.

"How'd you get the hideout?"

"I didn't," I said. "I don't have one."

"You bluffed him? Geez, Cruickshank, you must have balls of solid brass."

"There wasn't much choice. All I had was a bluff. Who is he anyway? At first, I thought he might be Dan-Dan himself, but when he mentioned the boss, it was clear that he wasn't."

"Describe him," Baca asked.

"Older guy, average height, say five nine or ten. Slim like he's fit, not just skinny. Gray hair with a full head of it, combed back in what they used to call a pompadour. Looks like his nose was broken about six times. Lot of attitude. Carries a Glock nine, or did until I took it away from him."

"Sounds like Mickey Dee," Baca said.

"Mickey Dee what?"

"Just Mickey Dee. Dee is his last name. He's Dan-Dan's number two guy. His best friend, too. They've known each other since they were kids. Dan-Dan's folks kind of adopted Mickey when his parents died in an automobile accident while in the old man's employ. They even look a little alike, which made people wonder if Danny might be Mickey Dee's daddy, too. That would help explain why he took the kid in. He's smarter than Dan-Dan, but that's like saying he's the tallest Munchkin. The big difference is that Mickey Dee is a genuine tough guy while Dan-Dan just thinks he is. For whatever reason, Mickey Dee still looks up to him. Always has. Maybe it's gratitude for the way Dan-Dan's father took him in, but I dunno. I'm sure the other guys you saw are on the O'Bannion team, too."

"Is everybody in this outfit old?" I asked. "What is this, the gang from AARP?"

"Don't get cocky," Baca said. "An old guy can shoot you just as dead as anybody else. Next time, if there is a next time, Mickey Dee won't be so easy. He'll be pissed, too. He underestimated you and you embarrassed him. He won't underestimate you again."

"Point taken," I said. "I assume this changes our plans for tomorrow. I don't want to make any trouble for you."

"I don't see why it would," Baca said. "They know you're around, so we have to be extra watchful. But we can do that. They don't know that we talked or where you're staying or Mickey Dee would have said something. He always did run his mouth too much. Remember what he said? They were surprised when you walked in and had you made right away? That means they didn't know you were around. He must have felt like he struck gold.

"After what happened, they won't expect you to stick around. They have such a high opinion of themselves that they'll probably figure that, having lost the element of surprise, you'll put some distance between you and them, like maybe go back to Cabo and come back later when they don't expect it, except they might try to get to you first. That's what I'd do.

"We really need to do something about your SUV, though. You can't drive around in it, and I wouldn't leave it at the bed-and-breakfast where it could be spotted."

I explained it was parked in the back, where no one could see it from the street, which I knew was a temporary solution.

"You're right, that's not good enough," Baca agreed. "Tell you what, once it gets dark, come back here. You can park it in my garage, where nobody can see it. I'll drive you back to the bed-and-breakfast and pick you up in the morning for our little tour."

"By the way, Eddie Heenan wants you to call him. Says it's important."

"Why didn't he call me himself?" I asked. "And how did he know to call you?"

"Beats me," Baca said. "Maybe he tried? Reception up here sucks sometimes. Then he tried me and got lucky."

We ended the conversation and I called Heenan. Reception would not have been better if he were in the next room.

"Baca said you called. What's up?"

"Just a second," he said, followed by a longish pause.

"Okay, open your door."

"What?"

"Open your door."

Feeling a little silly, I opened the door.

And there he was, phone in hand and a big grin on his face.

"I got the room next door," he said.

CHAPTER 31

HEENAN EXPLAINED in a rush of words.

"Barcelo called me after you two talked. He got the impression that you might try to lone wolf it up here and maybe that wasn't a great idea. I decided to come up without saying anything because you are a stubborn horse's ass. If I asked if you needed help, you'd say that you didn't, even if you did, so why bother to ask? There's a private airport in Tahoe and I flew in there."

I didn't bother to ask Heenan how he knew where I was staying because I was happy to see him. As reinforcements go, he's better than the cavalry.

But at the same time, I was cranky that Barcelo didn't mind his own business. I decided that I was a lot more pleased than cranky and let it go, thereby proving that I am not a stubborn horse's ass.

Heenan stepped into the room. I took a chair next to a little round table by the bay window. He settled into the chair on the other side of the table while I caught him up.

"Close one," he said with a shake of his head. "Good thing you sat where you did in that booth, or you never could have reached the guy's Glock."

Heenan was right. I was lucky. Sometimes that's all you need.

"So tomorrow we're gonna go see this castle thing?" he asked.

"Baca says it's still a go as far as he's concerned. In the meantime, if I don't get something to eat, I may start chewing on one of these stupid pillows. But first, I've got to call my digital nerd. She's looking into something that might have to do with all this. And then I've got to call my office manager because there's a problem at the agency she says only I can solve."

"It's nice to be needed," Heenan said. "Tell you what, while you make your calls, I'll go out and find us something to eat. You shouldn't risk being seen anywhere around here for a while."

I called Maria first. It was late enough that I called her at home. She said to call no matter when, though she liked to keep normal hours. Ursula was a night owl, so I could call her practically any time.

"*Jefe*, we have a client problem," she said. "Unbelievable as it seems, only you can fix it, wherever you are."

"Clients," I said. "Those pesky bastards."

It was a problem we had before, ever since I became Ethan Cruickshank, celebrity detective, or detective to celebrities, or whatever I was, and formed the agency. Three potential clients wanted me and only me to take on their cases. They weren't willing to settle for what one of them dismissed as "the B team," which was something I did not like to hear. In my agency, there was no B team.

When that happens, I usually explain that I can't do everything myself and our other detectives are as good as it gets, and if that isn't good enough, maybe they should look elsewhere. Goodbye.

But two of the three cases promised to be exceptionally lucrative, which is what happens when cases turn into lots of billable hours and the clients are people of means who can easily afford it, which always has a way of getting my attention.

"Okay," I said. "We'll play it as usual."

"I thought that's what you'd say," Maria said.

I made the calls. It was outside normal work hours, but it was a good way to show that the agency never sleeps.

And then I lied, which is what I meant by as usual.

Of course, I would take the case on myself, I said, three times in three different ways. I took the not-so-lucrative case because people of lesser means need detecting, too, and it helped soothe the tiny bit of guilt I felt for lying to the others. I promised to give all three cases my full personal attention. I would not rest until I saw them through, and blah, blah, blah, blah.

I did point out that I'd delegate some of the routine work to others, seeing how I was such a busy and important man. By routine work, I meant practically everything.

I took down preliminary information on my iPad and sent it to Maria's office email. "As usual" also meant that Mike and Antonio would do the early work and probably all or most of the rest of it.

Later, I would report to the clients in a document over my signature, which is what they wanted to see.

Don't ever tell me I have a B team. I'll respond with a big dose of "as usual."

CHAPTER 32

Ursula answered my call just as Heenan walked into the room with two bags stuffed with McDonald's food-like products.

"I Googled and found one, though it was kinda far," he said. "You can always count on McDonald's. I don't know what you like, so I got you a Big Mac and a Quarter Pounder, plus fries of course. And a little something for me. And a shake. You've got your choice of chocolate or vanilla. I'll take the other one."

The unmistakable McDonald's scent from the bags practically had me drooling. I told Ursula to hold on a second and took a mighty bite out of a Big Mac, chewing and sighing with pleasure at the same time.

"Ethan, what *are* you doing?" Ursula asked, not sure what to make of the sounds coming out of her phone.

"Eating a Big Mac. I was about to pass out from hunger."

Ursula responded with something in Portuguese that did not sound complimentary to either me or McDonald's. Most of the time, when she threw out insults, it was in her native language. She claimed to be more creative that way.

I was not deterred, and the Big Mac disappeared in a matter of seconds.

"Okay, crisis passed," I offered another contented sigh as I lifted the lid off my chocolate shake. "What's going on?"

"As you requested, I went over everything I could find on Donald Burnside's financials," she said. "It wasn't a deep dive, but I think it tells you what you need to know."

"And?"

"Burnside is seriously underwater, or should be. While he makes a nice salary from the state of New Mexico, he pays alimony to two ex-wives, plus child support to one. He spends a lot on clothes and vacations, and his credit cards are maxed out. His expenses exceed his income, but he never seems to cut back. He makes up the shortfall by withdrawing money from an offshore account in Singapore."

"Singapore?"

"Think of it as Switzerland in Asia, at least financially. Burnside is smart about it and only withdraws the money he needs to make up his shortfall so that he doesn't draw attention by transferring large amounts of money at one time. Right now, the Singapore account has a little more than three hundred thousand dollars in it. He has never moved more than ten thousand at one time, always just enough to keep his nose above water."

"Where does he get the money that goes into the Singapore account? Three hundred thousand is not a small potato for a guy who should be in serious financial trouble."

"Mostly transferred from other offshore accounts and dummy corporations concealed by the usual financial smokescreens," she said. "To answer your next question, what I think he's doing is selling information."

I thought it over. It made sense, though there were other possibilities.

"In Burnside's position, he would pick up a lot of chatter," I said. "Most of it worthless but some of it might be valuable to the right people, especially if he was somehow listening in on conversations between the prisoners and their family or lawyers, either in person or on the telephone, or to the many long conversations between the Feebs and one of the world's most successful assassins. That one alone could be a gold mine. He could sell the information to anybody from individuals to entire governments."

As I thought it over, Ursula issued a warning. "Ethan, please don't be too eager and do something based only on this information," she said. "I don't know if what I suspect is true. But the money is coming from somewhere, and he obviously wants to keep it hidden. It wasn't the money itself, but his spending habits that made it easy to find. I can't imagine what else he might possess that would be so valuable and paid for in such a way."

I couldn't either.

Maybe he was blackmailing somebody, or many somebodies?

But who and for what? And that didn't explain the range of the financial activity. According to Ursula, there were many different deposits from different sources. It was impossible for Burnside to be blackmailing that many people.

Peddling information was the better bet, with maybe a little blackmail on the side with the right information. If true, Donald Burnside was playing a dangerous game with dangerous people.

How long had this been going on?

I didn't care.

Sitting here thinking about it while I consumed my Quarter Pounder didn't move the needle. I decided to put Burnside away for now and attend to immediate business.

"Ursula, can you gin up something in an email, or text, or something? However you want to do it. Make it seem like I'm telling somebody at the office that I'll be back in Cabo late tomorrow so we can have a staff meeting the next morning, and then put it out there so that whoever is trying to spy on us will see it?"

"Of course, I can do misdirection," she said. "But they might be suspicious that this is the only communication of yours they were able to see and recognize it for what it is."

"I know, but I want to at least put the thought in their heads that maybe I really am headed back. With what happened today, they might be prepared to believe it."

"What happened?" she asked.

When I didn't answer right away, she knew that I didn't intend to answer at all. I wanted to keep the number of people who knew exactly what I was doing to a minimum. That way, if I got into trouble with the law, Ursula and others could rightfully claim they didn't know what I was up to.

"All right, Ethan, go ahead and be difficult," she grumped. "On this other thing, what if I mix the misdirection in with a lot of other nonsense and put it out there so that what we want them to see isn't the only thing they see? They might think we had a temporary security breach that we found and fixed."

"Perfect," I said. "Ursula, as ever, I thank you."

"It's what I do," she said. "If you won't answer a specific question, how about something general. How are things going? Everybody here worries about you."

Let's see, I thought, I flew from Cabo to Los Angeles

to Sacramento, rented an ugly SUV, drove into the Sierra Nevada foothills, met an ex-sheriff named Santiago Baca at his winery, drank wine and talked to Baca for a couple of hours about a dangerous gang of codgers, left Baca, checked into a bed-and-breakfast with lots of stupid pillows, got a restaurant recommendation, settled in for an early dinner, nearly got killed, disarmed the would-be killer and left him at the side of the road, went back to my bed-and-breakfast, talked to Baca for a little while, discovered that Eddie Heenan had the room next door, solved a minor crisis at the agency by lying extensively, talked to my digital nerd, who explained that a guy I once trusted, well, not entirely, probably was crooked, set up a plan to fool the bad guys, ate a sumptuous dinner of McDonald's finest, and the day wasn't over yet.

"Action-packed," I said.

CHAPTER 33

AFTER OUR ENTHUSIASTIC display of gastronomic calamity, in the darkness, I drove to Baca's place. Heenan followed to make sure that I didn't pick up a tail.

Baca had already moved his SUV out of the garage and left the door open so I could drive my rental in, close the door, and get it out of sight.

Baca and Heenan had talked on the phone but never met. I worried a little about how the two alpha males might play together. At first, they circled each other like two big dogs trying to figure out which one would lead the pack before each one decided that the other was okay and there was no pack to lead anyway.

After confirming that Baca would pick us up the next morning, we drove back to the bed-and-breakfast in Heenan's rented sedan. I was about as tired as I had ever been and caught myself dozing on the way.

I just barely made it upstairs to my room, where I ripped off my clothes, threw the irritating decorative pillows to the floor, put the Glock I'd taken from Mickey Dee under the bed where I could easily reach it, and gratefully eased under the covers.

Helluva day.

CHAPTER 34

AFTER DEVOURING the usual massive breakfast offered at such places, including orange juice and three cups of coffee for me and some kind of green, evil-smelling, health gunk for Heenan, Baca picked us up the next morning after cruising around for a while to make sure nobody was tailing him or watching the bed-and-breakfast.

I climbed into the rear seat of Baca's dirty white SUV, where it would be harder to see me from outside. With his size, Heenan was more comfortable in front anyway. His bulk also helped block the view if anybody tried to peer in.

To change my look, I wore a pair of aviator sunglasses and an old European Waterways cap left over from a vacation Dina and I took in France many years ago. On business, I always traveled with at least two hats and two pairs of sunglasses, all of them different from each other for multiple looks.

As the SUV rumbled away, Heenan asked, "How long 'til we get there?"

"About forty-five minutes," Baca said.

"You sure this old heap's gonna make it?"

Hands firm on the steering wheel at the two and ten o'clock positions, Baca's indignation rose on behalf of the old heap.

"It's not old, it's seasoned, and, yes, it will damn well make it! Almost two hundred and fifty thousand miles and I'd trust it to drive across the country and back a couple of times, smart guy. Would you rather hitchhike?"

"It might be faster," Heenan groused as we rattled down the road, swaying dramatically with every curve as if the SUV's twenty-year-old suspension might collapse at any moment. "Not to mention more comfortable."

Baca and Heenan had only met last night and already enjoyed needling each other. I shouldn't have worried.

"Okay, let's get down to business," Baca declared, eyeing me in the rearview mirror.

"Like I told Ethan yesterday, we'll only see a small part of the O'Bannion place from the road, but at least you'll get a feel for the weirdness of it. I hit up a friend this morning and cadged a half dozen photos of the place taken from a drone a while back. He emailed 'em to me and I printed them out. They're in the folder on the seat next to Ethan."

I sorted through the surprisingly high-quality photographs and felt my chin fall to my chest.

The word castle didn't really describe it. But no other word that I could come up with did either.

There were two large towers, one on each end, complete with parapets that made them look like medieval siege towers, as if the owner expected revolting peasants or some rival baron to storm the castle. The wall connecting the towers ran all the way around an inner courtyard. The walled area was longer side to side than front to back and covered so much ground that the drones either couldn't or didn't get high enough to get the front and rear wall in the same photograph.

The place even had a drawbridge, which was down when the photos were taken. The drawbridge passed over a ditch that seemed to run all the way around the castle, or whatever it was.

Inside the wall, among other bizarre details, the photos showed what appeared to be a larger-than-Olympic-size swimming pool adjacent to the main building, which was an awkward-looking combination of formidable citadel and comfortable château, like a French vacation home that was ready to withstand an invading army of thousands of unwanted relatives. The pool was complete with a two-story waterfall glistening in the sunlight while the area around the pool was decorated in some kind of goofy tropical theme. It looked like a tiki resort favored by the late Jimmy Buffett and his parrot-head fans somehow got mixed up with 15th-century France.

This clash of styles—towers, wall, pool, waterfall, château-citadel, and tiki bar surroundings—wasn't as monumental in size as the Hearst Castle in California, but it looked a lot more ridiculous, like the various parts were misplaced in time, with some of it built five hundred years ago and some of it the day before yesterday.

It was hard to tell from the drone shots, but outside the rear wall, it looked like the tree-covered land gradually sloped down toward Lake Tahoe in the far distance.

Until now, the Hearst Castle at San Simeon was the greatest monument I'd ever seen to what happens when someone with very little taste and a big ego has too much money. But in its way, the O'Bannion Castle was in a league by itself. Though smaller, with its mishmash of styles, it was grotesque in a way the Hearst Castle was not, and looked like the creation of some fevered nightmare after a too-spicy midnight pizza.

Driving by, we couldn't see that much from the road, just enough of the wall and towers to give the place a kind of wacky reality. There was a guard gate at the entrance, about fifty yards off the public road on a private lane leading to the castle. The barrier was down and a uniformed guard was standing beside the little guardhouse. Using the binoculars Baca conveniently left on the back seat, I saw a weapon holstered on the guard's right hip.

Baca drove slowly so we could get a good look. Once we were out of sight, he turned around for another pass, and I wondered if we might draw too much attention.

"Don't worry about it," he said. "People drive by here and gawk all the time. Sometimes they make three or four passes, or stop and take pictures. It's one of the biggest tourist attractions around here that's not really a tourist attraction."

I passed the folder to Heenan so he could take a look.

"Is it as macabre inside as out?" I asked.

"I've never been inside, but those who have say it is, maybe even worse, though that's kinda hard to believe," Baca said.

"Supposedly, the monstrosity was never finished because Ruthie kept changing her mind about her grand intentions. The original marble and granite were cut and shaped by Italian masons, as if anybody around here could tell the difference. The plans filed with the county back before construction began say it originally was supposed to have more than fifty rooms, eighteen fireplaces, and some two hundred windows, at least half of them genuine stained glass, and about two hundred thousand square feet altogether, including a three-story grand hall. The stairs and stairwells are mahogany, or were planned to be."

As we slowly passed by a second time, Baca shook his head at the madness of it all.

"It's been so long since anybody but O'Bannion associates and employees got inside that nobody really knows what's in there now," he said.

"For a guy like Danny O'Bannion, who you say didn't like to call attention to himself, I don't think I've ever seen a place that calls more attention to itself," I said. "How the hell did that happen?"

"Ruthie," Baca said. "Like I said yesterday, she was raised dirt poor someplace nobody ever heard of in Oklahoma, one of too many children in a family where incest was a way of life.

"For a kid, she must have had unbelievable drive and guts. She claimed that she got pregnant by her father at thirteen and didn't own a pair of shoes until she left home a year later. She got out as soon as she could, after somehow scraping up enough money to hop on a bus, and wound up in Tahoe because that was as far as her money took her, plus she figured nobody would look for her there. Remember that Tahoe wasn't that well-known yet. Even after the Olympics, most people got their sense of where it was from the burning map during the opening credits of *Bonanza*. Nobody knows what happened to the baby, if she had it. As far as I know, she never talked much about it."

"Geez, I remember that map," Heenan said. "I haven't thought of it in years."

"Yeah," I admitted, "me, too."

Ignoring our nostalgia indulgence, Baca continued his background briefing.

"Anyway, Ruthie looked older than she was and had a great body at a young age. First, she got a job as a coffee shop waitress, working where she didn't have to lie about her age. She was broke, and it was the first job she could get. Then she worked at a topless bar, where she lied to get the job and supposedly screwed the hell out of the owner. She dumped him the second she didn't need him anymore and the poor bastard committed suicide.

"She finally landed a gig as a showgirl, underage again. She literally remade and educated herself along the way. And that's when she met Danny O'Bannion. They married and became partners in everything.

"Within limits, Danny pretty much let her do anything she wanted while building this thing. When he suddenly died, it was only partially finished. With his death, supposedly she wanted to turn it into some kind of monument to her late husband, a man she genuinely idolized, but now that he wasn't around to control her whims it got out of hand, like she didn't know what she wanted and couldn't stop messing with it until it became an obsession.

"Danny would have been appalled by how it turned out, though he probably was appalled long before that. Ruthie was so smart at everything else, but absolutely nuts when it came to this."

The last item in Baca's folder was an architectural rendering of the whole place, including a large area outside the wall. Bumping and swaying along in Baca's SUV made it impossible to take it out and unfold it for a detailed look, so I saved it for later.

By now, we were headed back. Heenan and I were stunned into silence by what we'd seen and heard. Baca left us to our thoughts. It was almost too much to take in.

"So how many people live in this thing now?" Heenan asked, breaking the quiet as he so often did.

"I'm not sure," Baca said. "I don't think anybody is, though it's certainly not that many anymore. I guess there's Dan-Dan and whatever bimbo he's shacking up with, though it never lasts long. When he gets tired of 'em, he pays 'em off and makes sure they go away.

"We talked to one of 'em back before I retired, and she claimed that she was paid to be arm candy. Period. Dan-Dan's been married three times, but his exes aren't around anymore either. They took what money they got from the divorce and ran like hell."

Baca was his usual methodical self as he ran through the other possibilities.

"Let's see, probably Mickey Dee lives there, at least some of the time. Rudy used to live there but moved out when he started his drug-dealing catastrophe. He never married, so there's no widow. Dan-Dan might have some of his boys living there, too, maybe off and on, but I dunno for sure. It's been a while since the place was closely watched, and people kind of come and go, though there's much less of that now. It must take a helluva staff just for cleaning and maintenance, though they're probably all day workers.

"If Ethan's theory is right and Ruthie's still alive, she must be there, too. I don't know about medical care, like nursing or caregivers. And you saw the guard out front. There's somebody at that booth twenty-four seven. I don't know if there are others around the grounds, though I doubt it. I do know there's no guard gate anywhere else. That road is the only official way in."

"That's an awfully big place for not very many people, especially at night after the help goes home," I said. "Like you said yesterday, I'm not sure I would have believed it if I didn't see it for myself. If you didn't know your way around, you probably could get lost in there."

"Or hide, if you were so inclined," Heenan said, turning his head to give me a pointed look.

I had the same thought, stared back, and nodded.

Baca, who was driving and didn't see our exchange, added, "Hell, I've seen it plenty of times, at least from out here, and I still can't believe it."

"I wonder what that thing is worth?" I asked, not really expecting an answer.

"Probably not as much as you think," the business-savvy Heenan answered.

"For it to be worth anything, somebody else has to want it," he explained. "The land's worth something, of course, though it depends on zoning and what you could build there. But as to the rest of it, who'd want to buy something like that? I mean, what would you do with it? If you wanted to tear it down, clear it out, and build something new, it would cost a fortune before you even started building."

We drove in silence the rest of the way. What else was there to say?

CHAPTER 35

BACK AT THE E&S Winery, Baca produced a card table and three metal folding chairs. We opened them up in his cavernous wine storage room, or whatever winemakers called it.

With the big wine barrels in racks along the walls, even with the forklift to move the barrels around parked in the room, there was plenty of space for the table and chairs in the middle of the cool, temperature-controlled area. We had privacy, too. With no one there but the three of us, and Baca's son in the tasting room waiting on customers, we were unlikely to be disturbed.

We spread out the architectural drawing on the card table and stacked the photos next to it.

I asked if Baca had a magnifying glass. He went to his office and found one.

"Is there anything in particular you're looking for?" he asked.

"Yeah, a way out. An escape route, or tunnel, or something like it," I explained. "Somebody, probably Ruthie, the way it sounds, must have read up at least a little on European castles and palaces to get even a vague idea of what she wanted. Such places often had secret tunnels, a way for the nobles inside to come and go without being seen, which could be handy for someone like the O'Bannions if they were meeting people they didn't want other people to know about, which they probably did, given all the deal-making that went on.

"A tunnel also provided escape if things went south and you were under attack and not likely to hold out. For the O'Bannions, if the law suddenly showed up in force at the front door, they could get out the secret back way, though from what you say, it sounds like they never needed to. Most of the best-known castles in Europe have escape tunnels, and today they're just another part of the tourist attraction.

"Given the technology of the time, or lack of it, the tunnels weren't that long, just enough to get you outside and a bit away so you wouldn't be seen sneaking out. But with modern technology, for all practical purposes, there's no limit to how far you can go. And it wouldn't be hard to set up lighting inside the tunnel so you wouldn't break your leg in the darkness.

"Of course, the whole point of having a secret passage is secrecy. If the O'Bannions had one, I doubt that many people knew about it, mostly the workers who built it, and they may not have known exactly what they were building. By now, most of them have either died, retired, or moved away. I need to find a good map or some aerial photos showing the land all around this place, especially between the rear wall and the lake, if possible."

"Yeah, I see what you're thinking," added Heenan.

He got up from the chair and leaned over the table. With one hand flat on one side of the rendering, it looked as big as a frisbee, while the index finger on the other hand pointed out various possibilities.

"Maybe they had a boathouse with a fast boat down on the lake, or a vehicle concealed someplace near a dirt road that's not on any map? Or some kind of four-wheel thing that didn't need a road?

"If the way into the tunnel from inside was well hidden, then the opposition, whoever it might be, wouldn't know they were gone until they searched the whole place, and even then they'd have to find where the tunnel started and follow it to the end. All that would allow for a very nice head start. They could be well away before anybody knew they were gone. And if it's still there…"

Heenan and Baca looked at each other and, in unison, cried, "Google Earth." Being technologically primitive, the wonders of Google Earth, which I knew about but never used, hadn't occurred to me.

Our gathering also seemed a good opportunity to tell Baca that it was time for him to retire from our little team before he got in any deeper. He was already more involved than I wanted him to be. He was such a big help and enjoyed it so much that it was hard to shut him down. But it was time to call an end to it. I still didn't know exactly what I intended to do, or more likely, I was reluctant to face what I knew I had to do, but whatever happened, he should not be a part of it.

Naturally, he argued.

And naturally, I won.

His arguments to stay with us to the end were both emotional and logical, but as soon as I brought up his wife and son, this very good man knew that he had to give in and let us walk away.

I did have one more question.

Using the magnifying glass, on the architectural scheme, I spotted a faint red line that started inside the wall, somewhere inside the château-citadel. It went outside toward the lake, but seemed to peter out partway there. I couldn't tell if the line stopped, or if it originally went further but faded with age.

"Do you know what this is?" I asked, pointing at the thin line.

Baca practically put his nose on the rendering while he took a good look through the magnifying glass, tracing the line as best he could.

Rising up, he said, "Yeah, I remember from when we built the winery. The red line indicates some kind of water or sewer thing."

Baca bent over again for another look.

"It's strange, though. Back then, the O'Bannion place would either have hooked into the county system or installed its own well and septic tank."

"So what's strange?" I asked.

"The county system is in front, along the road, not in the rear. Always has been. That's if the county even had a system back then. But if the O'Bannions put in their own well and septic, why have it so far away? There's no point, and it's a lot more expensive. Plus, there's only one red line here. I'm no expert, but I doubt that you'd put your well and septic in the same place, or even running side by side. The county wouldn't want it too close to the lake either."

"Maybe the septic is along the red line but closer in, while the well is somewhere out there a ways along the same line," Heenan suggested. "Or vice versa?"

"I dunno," Baca said. "I'm just not seein' it. What would be the point? Of course, it was put in well before I built the winery, so maybe things were different then?"

"Maybe," I said.

CHAPTER 36

"You know what we need?" Heenan asked.

"The answer to that question would make a very long list," I said.

"No, really," he insisted. "We need a metal detector to help us find the tunnel exit out in the woods, assuming there is one. There's gotta be a door or something. If the door's not metal, there are certainly locks and hinges, which means metal, especially if it was installed a long time ago, before all that synthetic stuff came along that works just as well as metal."

"We should have one by this time tomorrow," I said. "Maybe sooner."

Surprised, Heenan asked, "How did you arrange that?"

"I've got one word for you: Amazon. It'll be delivered to Baca's place. I had to ask one more favor."

"Of course." Heenan laughed. "Amazon—the source of all things. But why just one when two would be faster?"

"One of us needs to keep watch while the other searches," I said. "Maybe O'Bannion has a guard patrolling out there? Baca doesn't think so, but we need to be alert to the possibility. What about electronic surveillance? We've gotta look out for that, too, though nothing I've seen from this gang indicates a high level of sophistication in that way. And what if some civilian out on a hike, or something, blunders onto us by accident? It could cause complications. Whoever's watching can steer the hiker away.

"We can't watch for all that with both of us walking around staring at the screen of a metal detector, or wearing earphones so we can't hear anything else while waiting for it to go beep, or whatever those things do."

We were in our new digs, on the front porch, taking in the mellow dusk. I had a Black Bush Irish whiskey on the rocks about half consumed while Heenan was working on his second glass of Pinot Grigio.

Although I hoped that my bit of misdirection with Ursula worked and whoever was trying to spy on us was convinced that I high-tailed it back to Cabo after my experience with Mickey Dee, we decided that the bed and breakfast just wasn't secure enough. It was too open, and there were too many ways to approach it.

We searched for possibilities and found an Airbnb in North Lake Tahoe. There was only one way in and nothing in sight but tall pine trees and shade, but it was still convenient to get where we needed to go with ease and speed.

Heenan drove my SUV into Tahoe and returned it to the rental company. It cost more to turn it in there instead of Sacramento, where I rented it, but we might have to leave in a hurry and didn't want to worry about it. He Ubered back to the new place.

I still had to stay out of sight, so Heenan went on a shopping expedition to get supplies for a few days. Now we had nothing to do but wait until we got word from Baca that our Amazon delivery had arrived.

"I assume you have a plan once it gets here and we figure out how to use it?" Heenan asked.

He was sitting on a cheap web-bottom chair with his long legs crossed at the ankles on the porch railing. I was on the other side of a glass-topped table in a padded rattan chair. Nothing matched in this place, but we didn't care as long as the beds were comfortable and the appliances worked. It was so cool in the mountains that we didn't even need to turn on the air conditioner.

"Of course, I have a plan."

"Let me guess," he said, steepling his fingers in front of his chin. "You're pretty sure that the red line represents an escape tunnel. So we try to find an old tunnel that may or may not exist by blundering around in the woods and hope to get lucky with the metal detector. Then, if we can, we break open the door, or whatever it is, and hope that it doesn't set off some loud and nasty signal. We climb in and shuffle along in the dark while trying not to fall and bust our butts.

"Now, assuming all that works out, eventually we get inside the wall and into the main building, where we try to find a way out of the tunnel to where we're not sure so we can do what we both know has to be done in a place that has so many rooms we could wander around for a long time before finding anything, all while carefully avoiding people who may or may not be there until we discover the real object of our affection."

Heenan unsteepled his fingers, seized his wineglass, and raised it, along with his eyebrows. "Is that about it?"

"You have it right down to the last intricate, finely honed detail," I said.

After a long silence, I asked, "Have you ever used a metal detector?"

"Nope. Have you?"

"Never."

"We're screwed," he said.

"Nah," I said. "We'll think of something."

"Yep," he said. "It may not be the right thing, or the smart thing, but it'll be something."

CHAPTER 37

IT WASN'T THAT HARD.

After breakfast the next morning, we cleaned and checked our weapons to make sure they were in good working order. I had the Glock I'd taken from Mickey Dee, complete with a full 15-round magazine. Heenan carried a Smith & Wesson with seventeen rounds.

That should be more than enough. If we had to fire more than thirty-two shots, everything that could go wrong already did. Success depended on stealth getting in, enough time to find who we wanted, and speed getting out.

A little luck might come in handy, too.

Baca sent a text saying that the Amazon package arrived and he'd leave it in his garage with the door open. We could pick it up and be on our way in seconds.

As we headed out the door to pick up the metal detector, Heenan stopped me with a big hand on my shoulder. As we faced each other, his usual casual attitude disappeared, replaced by the thoughtful man I knew him to be beneath the surface frivolity.

"Ethan, we're getting down to it now, so I guess this is

as good a time as any to ask you one last question," he said.

"Are you sure, absolutely sure, you're ready to do this? I don't mean break into the place, if we can. I mean killing the bastards when we do. And not just the intended target, but everyone we run into. We can't leave behind anybody who can ID us, good or bad, guilty or innocent. I can do that, but can you?"

I didn't agree with everything he said, but the serious question deserved a serious answer.

"I've thought about it ever since you, Chango, and Valencia walked through the door to my condo that morning. I didn't know what I'd find when I started looking, or where the trail might lead, but it didn't matter. Despite what I said at the time, I realize that I was sure even then that I'd do whatever it takes, just as I'm sure now. Is that enough for you?"

Heenan nodded. We'd known each other a long time. That was all he needed.

Although Heenan was right, despite what I said, I was pretty sure that I couldn't kill the innocent along with the guilty, though it might be hard to tell one from the other. Dina would never forgive me. Come the time—if that time came—I knew I had to find another way, but I had no idea what it might be. All I could do was hope that I'd know it when I saw it.

From the beginning, this whole operation was one massive improvisation. Why stop now?

* * *

WHAT LITTLE ASSEMBLY the metal detector required was easy. A trial run showed that the LED screen was simple to read. According to the instructions, the detector could find something as small as a quarter even a couple of feet down. The fact that what we were looking for almost certainly would be covered by a blanket of dirt, pine needles, and who knew what else shouldn't pose a problem. All we had to do was slowly walk along and sweep the flat detecting end back and forth, which was easy enough since the apparatus was surprisingly light and came with a harness that was simple to slip on and off.

The problem was location. Where was that magic door? We had to approximate what we thought might be the location of the red line, using Google Earth, follow it as best we could to find the way in, and proceed from there.

We kept the metal detector on silent mode because we didn't want any beeping to give us away. The screen and vibrations would tell us when we were onto something.

The first day, we parked Heenan's rental car well off the side of a two-lane road and walked a mile and a half into the woods to the starting point. We'd seen cars parked on roadsides all around Lake Tahoe, presumably people out for a hike, a picnic in the woods, or a scenic photo opportunity, so one more shouldn't stand out.

The worst that could happen is that we might get towed, but more than likely, a warning left on the windshield would come first, followed by a ticket, if that. Tahoe liked to be kind to its tourists. That's where the money was.

We couldn't start close to the wall and risk being seen, so we based our starting position on the approximate location of the red line and the pictures from Google Earth. We slowly crossed and recrossed what we hoped might be the line's path while sweeping the metal detector back and forth, constantly making adjustments as we moved along.

We worked in hour-long shifts, the better to keep our concentration high. The one who wasn't working with the metal detector made wide three-hundred-and-sixty-degree sweeps, looking for electric surveillance, security from the castle, or some innocent character out doing nothing much except maybe tending the marijuana plants we spotted from time to time.

The first day we found seven beer and two soft drink cans.

It was too early in the search to be discouraged, so we weren't.

Disappointed? Yes.

* * *

WE SETTLED onto the deck of our cabin for an early evening drink. "Look on the bright side," I said. "At least we know the thing works."

"Yeah, maybe we could go into the recycling business?" Heenan scoffed.

* * *

WE AGREED that leaving the rental car at the side of the road, even if it was out of sight, wasn't a good idea, certainly not on successive days. We didn't want anybody, especially not law enforcement, to wonder why we parked there again, or assume that something was wrong and come looking for us.

Heenan drove into Lake Tahoe early on the second day, turned in his car, and rented a small SUV with four-wheel drive that we could take deeper into the woods. It easily took both of us, the metal detector, and two backpacks loaded with water, flashlights, energy bars, a few basic tools, and four pairs of gloves—two pairs of work gloves and two of surgical gloves, which would keep us from leaving fingerprints once we got inside and still allow us to use our weapons freely if we had to. Work gloves were too thick and cumbersome.

The second day produced eleven more cans, plus $1.35 in change, a gold earring, and a big silver belt buckle with a turquoise buffalo embedded in it, suitable for wearing at the rodeo.

* * *

As we regarded the day's findings during our now routine drink at dusk, I balanced the heavy belt buckle in my hands.

"There's probably an interesting story about why this was out there," I said. "These things don't come cheap."

"You know what they say," Heenan said.

"I can hardly wait," I said.

"Never let your daughter marry a man whose belt buckle is bigger than her head."

"Good parenting advice," I said.

CHAPTER 38

WE WON the grand prize on the third day.

It happened on my shift with the metal detector. It began to vibrate with more force than it had shown with any of the other junk we found. At the same time, the screen indicated that there was something big not far below the surface.

I stopped, took a deep breath to steady myself, then moved ahead very slowly, with the metal detector swinging from side to side. When the vibrations stopped, I turned around and walked back, a step to one side of my previous path. I wanted to get a sense of the size of what I'd found.

Whatever it was, it was a whole lot bigger than a beer can or a belt buckle.

I finally came up with something that was roughly four by eight, apparently most or all of it metal. The dimensions seemed about right for what I hoped it might be.

I stopped, pulled off one work glove, and flicked the sweat off my forehead with my index finger. Then I pulled out my phone and speed dialed Heenan.

Speaking in a whisper, I said, "Got something. Do you know where I am?"

"Hell yes, I know where you are. I've been walking circles around you for forty-five minutes. I'm on my way."

For a big man, Heenan could move as quiet as a ghost when he wanted to. He suddenly appeared at my side without my hearing a sound.

I told him what I found and loosely marked out where it was with my foot.

"Let's work outside in and keep our body weight outside the edges as much as possible, at least at first," I said.

"If it really is our way in, we don't know how stable it is after all these years. I know it can take my weight because I stupidly walked over it with the metal detector, but I don't know about both of us. After all this work, we don't want to announce ourselves by falling into the bat cave like some kind of comedy act."

"Well, this is another fine mess you've gotten us into," Heenan said.

"Eddie, your Oliver Hardy is a lot better than your Bogart."

With me on one side of the defined area and Heenan on the other, using ordinary garden spades, we got down on our hands and knees to work around the outside edge, sweeping and pushing and yanking away the weeds, needles, branches, dirt, and detritus of decades. Some of it was hard and some of it easy, but we made steady progress.

At the first glimpse of rusty metal battered by the years, Heenan whispered, "Well, by God, I think we found it."

CHAPTER 39

AFTER CLEARING the edges all the way around, we backed away. I needed a moment to think.

If it was what we were looking for—and Heenan was right, what else could it be?—we still had at least another couple of hours work to clear the entire surface before trying to open what appeared to be a large metal door similar in size to what you'd find to get into the basement of a Kansas farm house to escape a tornado.

Once we had the door cleared, should we make our move and go in, or wait until darkness?

Could we even get inside? It was not a sure thing.

Assuming we could, both possibilities had pros and cons. We could see better in the daylight, but down in the tunnel, once we closed the door behind us, day or night probably wouldn't make much difference. Even if there was lighting installed, I didn't want to use it and possibly alert anyone in the castle.

There was a good argument in favor of moving fast to get this thing over with before anybody discovered what we were doing.

But if we waited until late night, by then the daytime help inside the castle, assuming there was some, would have gone home, reducing the number of people we might encounter. People were less alert late at night, too, which would be to our advantage.

I settled on a compromise. We'd finish clearing off the door and assess the difficulty involved in cracking it open. If it looked like we could do it with reasonable ease, we'd go back to our place, try to catch a few hours' sleep if we weren't too wired, eat something, then return late tonight.

Leaving the door revealed for anyone to see was a risk. But in the three days we spent looking, not a soul had come by. We could hide the door with some of the fallen tree branches we'd seen all over the place during our search for the door. Unless they were looking for it specifically, if anyone walked by, chances are they wouldn't see it.

Could we find our way back in the dark?

We could. Plus, as Heenan pointed out, we could use the GPS in our phones to get us here, then use the flash-lights we had in our backpacks to confirm our position.

I didn't want to use the lights built into our phones because I didn't want to run down the batteries. I sure as hell didn't want to try to communicate with somebody in an emergency and be stymied by a dead phone.

So we continued to clear our little garden. Everything would happen tonight.

One way or the other.

CHAPTER 40

IT WAS JUST about midnight when we broke in.

To my surprise, I actually managed to get an hour's sleep. Heenan got some sleep, too. I heard him snoring in the other bedroom.

We drove within a half mile with the SUV, turned it around, and pointed it in the direction we had come from in case we had to leave on the run.

Walking carefully and quietly, we made our way to the door. This was no time to twist an ankle. Even in the darkness of the woods at night, the location was easy to find. We stopped about twenty-five yards away and waited for ten minutes to make sure nobody was out there waiting for us.

From what we'd seen earlier, the hinges looked like the weak spot. They'd rusted over time so that, with a little muscle, we were able to pop off both hinges with a small crowbar.

Fortunately, the screech of breaking metal we feared was more of a groan. Even so, we moved away and waited again to make sure the noise didn't attract attention.

With me on one side and Heenan on the other, we

lifted the heavy metal door off the entrance, set it aside, and contemplated the gaping hole.

"We've gotta take a look down there to see what we're getting into," I whispered.

With one gloved hand over the top of the flashlight so that most of the beam shined down rather than out, Heenan kneeled at the edge. We saw ten concrete steps leading down to a flat surface that appeared to go toward the castle in a straight line. The tunnel, at least this part of it, was about eight feet wide.

I flicked on my own flashlight and we moved the beams around the tunnel passage, walls, and ceiling. What we mostly saw were cobwebs. The tunnel was thick with them.

"We don't want to walk through that in the dark," Heenan whispered. "That crap would distract us with every step. Makes it kinda creepy, too. I never liked that stuff."

"The good news is that the cobwebs indicate that nobody comes down here, at least not very often," I said. "We can get a couple of branches off the ground, wave them in front of us, and knock that stuff down as we go. Every so often, we'll use one of the flashlights to make sure we're not about to fall down any steps, or something.

"Be careful not to move too far with each step and make sure of firm footing every time. Slow but safe. Using the flashes occasionally should give us a better sense of perspective, too."

We searched around and found a couple of small branches for cobweb control. Then we found several bigger branches, thick with dead foliage and needles, and laid them over the door. We climbed inside so that we were standing on the steps. As quietly as we could, we muscled the door back over the hole.

It wasn't perfect, but it would do at night. If we weren't out by morning, something had gone terribly wrong.

Another look around showed bare light bulbs on the ceiling, but no sign of a switch.

"It's probably at the other end," I said. "Remember, this was mostly for escape or a way to get somewhere in secret. If we have to go that far in, we should try to find the switch so we can light the tunnel in case we have to leave in a hurry."

"That'll probably let 'em know we're here," Heenan warned.

I shrugged. "If we're in that much of a hurry, there's a good chance somebody's chasing us."

We turned off the flashes, eased down the steps, and began moving forward, waving the branches as we went to fend off the cobwebs. Our progress was faster than I thought it would be. Despite our efforts, twice I took cobwebs full in the face, stopped in my tracks, and almost frantically brushed them away.

Heenan was right. It was creepy, especially in the dark.

After almost an hour, with tension pressing on us like a heavy weight, we took a break and used the flashlights for a quick look around. The tunnel was still straight as a plumb line. To our relief, there seemed to be fewer cobwebs, too.

Heenan swallowed a big gulp of water, washed it around in his mouth, and spat it out.

"Does that mean somebody's been down here fairly recently?"

"I dunno," I admitted. "A couple of times in the last few minutes, I thought I felt a little air circulation. The movement of the air might keep 'em from forming in the first place."

"Where would air movement come from down here?"

"I don't know that either. Maybe we're getting close and it's air escaping around the doors into the castle if they're not a perfect fit, like they're warped, or something. Or maybe they've just got some air circulation going closer to the castle?"

We started moving again in our world of darkness, unseen cobwebs, our own heavy breathing, our footsteps constantly shuffling on the concrete, the musty, earthy smell that seems to belong to all tunnels, no matter what they're made of, cigarette smoke, the occasional scrabbling of some small creature like a mouse or rat getting out of our way...

Cigarette smoke?

I reached out into the darkness and stopped Heenan in his tracks.

"Do you smell cigarettes?" I whispered.

I could hear Heenan's long, shallow breathing.

"Maybe," he said. "Hard to tell, though. Might just be your suggestion."

"Look for a glimmer of light, however small, that might come in from a badly fitting door with a room on the other side," I said. "More than likely at the top or bottom."

Starting on the right, I crawled around on the floor while Heenan, who was four inches taller than my six two, examined the top while we tried not to bump into each other in the darkness.

A few minutes later, we found it.

CHAPTER 41

"GOT IT," Heenan whispered.

I rose from my knees and stood beside him.

It was too dark to see where he was pointing. He fumbled around until he found my wrist and moved my hand up the wall and slightly to the left.

"Right above your hand," he said. "See it?"

I stepped closer, stood on tip-toe, practically put my nose on the wall, and looked up to where I thought Heenan meant.

I saw it, too. It was just barely visible, but it was there.

I got back down on my knees and shuffled a couple of feet to the right. Now that I knew that something should be there, I saw it. Another faint hint of a glimmer that had no reason to be there except for light on the other side.

It was as if a door sagged fractionally to the left, leaving a tiny gap on the upper left and lower right. The hinges probably started working loose with age.

Whispering so quietly I could barely hear myself, I said, "Feel around for a knob, or anything you might grab to open a door."

This time, I was the one who found it, a leather loop

about waist high, directly below where Heenan first saw the light.

"It pulls open from this side," I whispered. "I bet you can just push it open from the other side. If it's flush to the wall in there, that would make it harder to see."

"How would they close it from that side?"

"Probably some kind of grab that doesn't look like it. Like a decoration or something. Or maybe something you press."

"I'll go in first," I said. "You hang back so if some-body's in there, they won't see you if I get into trouble."

I pulled the Glock from its position at the small of my back and heard the rustle when Heenan drew his Smith & Wesson.

"Ready," I said.

"Yes."

I gently pulled the leather strap. The door stuck, so I reluctantly tugged a little harder. The result was a wood-on-wood scraping that I didn't want to make.

Sliding inside the barely open door, I took a moment to get my bearings. The lighting was dim, but compared to the pitch black of the tunnel, it was like high noon on the Sahara.

I was at the back of what appeared to be a walk-in closet that was bigger than some studio apartments, stuffed with so much clothing it was impossible to shrug my shoulders without jostling something. Some of it was hanging in aged garment bags or covered in brittle plastic, and some of it wasn't.

Without close examination, I had the impression that it was women's clothes. I am no expert, but even I could tell that a lot of it was from a distant time.

My movement in the closet as I brushed through the hanging clothes released a scent that combined moth balls, at least what I thought I remembered what moth balls smelled like, mold, and age, as if the contents had been hanging undisturbed for a long time.

But even stronger than that was what I smelled earlier in the tunnel—cigarettes, but not just cigarettes. It was much more, and much more awful.

It was thousands and thousands of dead cigarettes and cigarette filters, a lifetime of smoking releasing clouds of smoke resulting in a stench that permeated the walls, ceiling, and carpet, if there was any, along with ashes left spilling over in ashtrays for far too long.

There was a sick smell, too, or maybe the smell of sickness, of many medications over many years combined with a stunning lack of hygiene for a remarkably long time.

Even in the closet jammed with the old clothes and their own peculiar scent, the stench from the room that must be on the other side was a fearsome thing. My eyes were watering and I wasn't even there yet.

Put it together and what did I have?

I was in a big walk-in closet that probably adjoined the bedroom of an old lady in poor health, who lived like a pig, smoked like a fire pit, never threw anything away, and didn't get out much, or at all.

CHAPTER 42

IT TOOK a while to find the other end of the closet.

I tried crouching, but the closet was as thick with clothes down low as it was higher. I couldn't see more than six inches in front of my face.

Assuming that the door to the tunnel was in the back, I fumbled my way toward the front, rustling clothes and hangers as I went. The weak light came from ceiling outlets with light fixtures that had the sleek look of something considered modern in the 1950s or early '60s. I had the feeling that the lights had been on for a very long time.

I felt the closet end in double doors before I actually saw it and almost bumped into it.

I waited, listened, and heard nothing. Then I waited some more.

Still nothing.

"Anything," whispered Heenan, who had entered the closet but kept to the rear where he couldn't be seen.

"Nothing. I'm going in."

"Be careful. If you need help, I can't move that fast in this mess. Lemme get a little closer."

Rustling sounds.

"Okay, that's better. I'm about three feet behind you. Go when you feel it. I'll step up a little when you do."

With the Glock in my right hand held down by my knee, I lowered the door handle with my left and slowly opened one of the double doors a fraction.

I couldn't see anything that mattered, though I did get the sense of a bedroom big enough to satisfy the needs of Marie Antoinette and decorated in similar fashion. What little I could see looked like a not very well-tended museum exhibition.

I opened the door just enough to slide through sideways.

"Hello, asshole. Why don't you bring your friend in, too?"

CHAPTER 43

AT FIRST, I didn't see the source of the voice.

To the right, at one end of the big, high-ceilinged room, was a four-poster bed that was roughly the size of Staten Island.

The dry scratch of a voice seemed to come from the bed, though I wasn't sure until I stepped closer and saw movement. Now that I was deeper into the room, the stench was so overpowering I wished I'd brought a gas mask.

She was dwarfed by the bed. I doubt that she weighed more than seventy-five pounds. She was propped up on thick pillows, the pillow covers turned yellow with age. Her face was in partial shadow and I couldn't see it very well. Her hair was white and there wasn't much of it. It seemed to cling to her veined skull in wisps. Blankets came up to her bony chest.

When she shifted in the bed, I finally saw her features clearly. Her parchment skin and wrinkled face had the caved-in look common to someone who no longer has their teeth, as if her face collapsed in on itself. Outside the blankets, her skinny arms looked like old leather stretched over bone. The bones in her wrists and elbows stood out like doorknobs.

At the end of those raised arms, two skeleton hands were clasped around a Colt Python, a weapon suitable for rhinoceros hunting that was pointed at me. The way she held it told me that she knew how to use it.

"Put your gun on the floor and tell whoever came with you to get their ass in here, too. Now!"

"You hear that?" I asked, kneeling to lay the Glock on the floor.

"Yeah."

"Come on in."

"Why give it up?"

"'Cause I'll shoot your friend in the guts if you don't," she announced.

As Heenan emerged from the closet, I stepped up and to the right. Seeing my movement, he went left.

Though we were at the foot of the big bed, we were now at the corners, with enough separation that she couldn't cover both of us. In her condition, she could barely cover one of us. The heavy Python was too much weapon. Her arms already trembled with the weight, even though she was using both hands.

The tough old bird fought it as long as she could.

"Goddamn! Goddamn! Goddamn!" she screamed as her arms collapsed and her hands fell helplessly to her lap.

I was beside her in two long strides and slipped the Python out of her clutches. She was too feeble to resist. Just getting that close made me shiver.

I stepped back, transferred the Python to my left hand, and scooped up the Glock from the floor with my right.

And so I met the fabled Ruthie Koslow O'Bannion.

Rage burned in her watery eyes as she looked up from her hands, taking in both of us.

"I told my worthless shit of a son that the Python was too much for me. But when did he ever listen?"

"How'd you know we were here?" I asked.

"I heard the door scrape when you came in from the tunnel. Then you clumsy bastards sounded like a couple of elephants loose in the closet."

She took a hard look at Heenan.

"I don't know you," she said.

She gave me the same treatment, only the look lingered.

"But I do know you. I never forget a face. You're the bastard who killed my baby grandson. You're supposed to be dead."

"Not hardly," I said.

CHAPTER 44

"So what now?" Heenan asked.

The answer came boiling through the door with Dan-Dan and his buddy Mickey Dee, both of them armed.

I glanced at the old lady. She raised one claw. There was a buzzer in it. She must have had it at her side in the bed and used it after I took the Python.

There we were, a merry gang of five.

I had my gun on Dan-Dan, Heenan had his on Mickey Dee, and Dan-Dan and Mickey Dee returned the favor.

The loving mother turned her kind attention to her beloved son.

"You told me you killed him, but it looks like you were wrong, as usual. Or maybe you were just lying again? So what the fuck happened, stupid?"

"Ma, I said I *had* him killed. I never said I did it myself."

"Yeah, yeah, yeah. In other words, you screwed up again. The only thing I can rely on in this world is that you will always let me down. All these years and you're still the same old meat-headed shit sack who can't do anything right!"

"Ma! I've asked you a thousand times, please, don't talk to me like that in front of...in front of...people!"

Dan-Dan was practically squirming on his feet with humiliation. He wasn't giving an order, or even asking. He was whining and pleading with Mommy like a little boy, something he probably did all his life to the mother who detested him for reasons probably neither one of them ever understood.

Even Mickey Dee seemed embarrassed, though, as Dan-Dan's closest friend, he'd probably seen it before. It was something you could see every day of your life and never get used to it.

"Oh, shut up and grow a pair, you stupid fuck! If you were—"

The three shots came so close together they were almost one.

Dan-Dan shot his mother.

I shot Dan-Dan.

Heenan shot Mickey Dee, who died looking surprised at the whole thing, like he expected Dan-Dan to stand there and take it like he always did.

In the big room, the concussive effect was massive. It felt like the shots might bring the walls down.

My shot was a little off thanks to using an unfamiliar weapon that once belonged to Mickey Dee. Shot in the chest, Dan-Dan was still alive. Barely.

Flat on his back, he feebly reached out toward his friend.

"Mickey, I'm sorry," he choked. "She wouldn't stop. I couldn't take it any..."

And then he died.

"Jesus," muttered Heenan.

And I came to life.

"Eddie, check where they came in. See if anybody's coming."

Eddie hustled out the door that Dan-Dan and Mickey Dee entered. I went over to the bed. Dan-Dan's shot didn't just kill his mother, it destroyed her. It wasn't a body in the bed. It was a small pile of bones and useless flesh, and not much of that. It wasn't even bleeding.

I checked Dan-Dan and Mickey Dee, though I knew it wasn't necessary.

After a few minutes, Heenan re-entered the bedroom, shaking his head.

"Not a soul," he said. "I went down the hall and down the big staircase. Nothing. This place, at least what I saw of it, feels empty. I'd bet on it."

"We may have to," I said. "What about the guard out front? Baca said somebody's there twenty-four seven."

"I'll take a look," he said.

I went over everything in the room again while Heenan was gone. He was absent long enough that I had started to worry when he popped back through the door.

"I got pretty close. He's still in his little guardhouse. He's got a big pair of earphones on and he's jiving like he's listening to music. He probably didn't hear a thing, given the earphones, the size of this place, and the location of the guardhouse. There are lots of thick walls between us and him.

"I can take him out easy, but I don't think it's necessary. Besides, if I do, the first person who comes in will see that the guard's down and know something's wrong. We'll buy more time if we leave him alone."

"I think it's time to go," I said. "What about you?"

Heenan looked around. "Yeah, let's get the hell outta here."

CHAPTER 45

I HAD WORKED out what to do while Heenan was checking on the guard.

We had three bodies. Dan-Dan shot his mother with his own gun. I shot Dan-Dan with a gun that used to belong to Mickey Dee. It might or might not be registered. Probably not. Either way, it didn't matter. Heenan shot Mickey Dee. Mickey Dee never had a chance to shoot anybody. I still had the Python that I took from the old lady.

Though we were wearing the surgical gloves, I grabbed a towel I found in the putrid en suite bathroom, wiped down the Glock I took from Mickey Dee, and put it in the old lady's dead hand. I put the Python in my waistband in case we ran into trouble on the way out.

"I assume your gun is clean," I asked Heenan.

"Absolutely," he said. "No way to trace it. But what you just did won't fool forensics for a second."

"I know, but it might add a little confusion. They'll know that Dan-Dan shot Mommy Dearest. But if she didn't shoot Dan-Dan, then who did and why stage it so that the weapon was in her hand? If it's registered to Mickey Dee, that should muddy things up a little, too.

And who shot Mickey Dee? Not to mention, where did everybody go, and how the hell did they get in here in the first place?"

"They'll figure it out eventually," he said. "At least some of it."

"Eventually can be a long time," I said.

* * *

GETTING out was a lot easier than getting in.

We didn't have to be careful or quiet. We made sure that the door leading out of the closet and into the tunnel was tightly shut when we left. We used our flashlights all the way as we dashed through the tunnel. We didn't care if we left footprints. We both wore desert boots with no pattern on the bottom. All the police might learn was our shoe size.

Climbing out of the tunnel, we put the door back in place and took care to camouflage the hell out of it. It was almost as well hidden as it was when I found it with the metal detector.

We practically ran all the way to the SUV as we stumbled through the woods. I used a rake we brought to erase the tire marks where we parked. The ground was hard and so thick with pine needles that I was sure we wouldn't leave tracks on the way out to the road. Everything was clear as we drove back to the cabin.

CHAPTER 46

WE WERE SO WIRED that we decided to keep going.

I started packing and wiping down everything while Heenan left the cabin to get rid of his Smith & Wesson and the Python.

When Heenan returned, he packed his own stuff as he explained, "I took 'em apart and scattered the pieces. If anybody finds anything, it'll be a hundred years from now."

We carefully followed the instructions the owner provided to leave the cabin, leaving nothing to call attention to ourselves. We weren't supposed to be out for another couple of days, but the owner wouldn't know that we left early. As requested, Heenan would send a text on the morning we were supposed to leave, telling him we'd just left. He'd never know the difference.

Still jazzed from what we'd done, we tossed the tools and backpacks, threw everything else in the SUV, and headed west on Highway 50 to Sacramento. We carefully wiped the SUV down before Heenan turned it in at the airport, paying the usual penalty for returning a rental somewhere other than where he rented it.

We split up. Heenan flew to Los Angeles and I flew to

Phoenix, then on to Cabo after a three-hour wait. I was lucky and got the last available seat on both flights, which meant that I was in the dreaded middle seat all the way. I endured.

I was still too wired to sleep, though I pretended I was sleeping to keep from talking to anyone.

After the usual long line to re-enter Mexico at the Cabo airport, I recovered my luggage and caught a taxi to my condo. I left my bag on the floor, drank two Bohemias in record time, took off my shoes, fell on the bed still wearing my clothes, and slept for twelve hours.

When I finally woke up, my eyes felt like they were glued shut and I sincerely wished that I hadn't fallen asleep in my clothes.

A long, hot shower solved every problem except hunger, which I took care of by throwing together a few odds and ends left in the refrigerator that mercifully hadn't gone bad. I hoped.

Following the plan I formed during the flight home, I called Baca, using vague language to tell him how much I enjoyed meeting him, not to mention the tour of his winery, and to ask what was going on, as if I was using it as a conversation starter.

He played along. "Funny you should ask. There were three killings up at Tahoe. We haven't had that kind of thing happen in a long time. The word is that it might be a gang thing, and by gang, they mean old-style mob, like long-delayed revenge, or something. Robbery is a possibility, too. The victims, one of them more than the others, were kind of famous in their day, wealthy with what they used to call ill-gotten gains.

"I think nobody's gonna be lookin' too hard since nobody's gonna miss the victims and it looks like the motive might be rooted in the past. Everybody'll do their jobs, of course, but nobody's gonna take the case on as a hobby. All three had well-known backgrounds, but that was a helluva long time ago. They were pretty much off the radar for a long time."

"I don't associate Tahoe with that kind of thing," I said.

"Nobody does anymore, though we'd probably be surprised at how many bodies are at the bottom of the lake. This area does have a kind of a colorful history. So what's up with you?"

I explained that the real reason for my call is that I wanted to follow up on our conversation when I visited the winery.

Once again, Baca didn't know what I was getting to, but he went along with it.

"You remember that you talked about wanting to make some improvements or additions but you weren't quite ready?" I said.

"Yeah."

"I'd like to invest in your operation so you can do that now instead of later. That's the real reason I was up there. A friend touted your operation, and I wanted to check it out without letting you know so I'd get the real skinny."

I hoped that Baca would go for it because it would tie up some loose ends. He wanted to put in a little food operation, plus a couple of other things he'd like to add to E&S, but didn't have the money yet. I wanted to repay him for being such a big help, but obviously I couldn't just hand him a bunch of money and say thanks for helping us kill three people who richly deserved it. I needed a legitimate reason.

Investigating a potential investment explained what I was doing up there in the first place, especially if I followed up with real money. Nobody could say it was a made-up excuse. It seems reasonable that I went up there to check it out, liked what I saw, and made an offer. The perfect cover.

Baca picked up on what I was doing, though he was reluctant to take the money. After explaining that I would not have, nor did I want, any say in the operation, and that I knew nothing about wine making anyway, he agreed.

"Look at it this way: I am investing in you," I explained. He liked the sound of that. "Besides, it kind of tickles me to invest in a winery."

"A lot of amateurs feel that way," he said. "Right up to the time when they lose their money,"

"I'll take my chances."

We settled on $100,000, with an option for another $50,000 down the road. I didn't think a contract was necessary, but he insisted on it to work out the details and in case something happened to either one of us.

One down and one more to go.

CHAPTER 47

MY NEXT CALL was to Chango Suarez.

I said nothing about Lake Tahoe, but did tell him what Ursula learned, or at least strongly suspected, about Burnside and his extra-curricular activities.

"I'm sure Ursula can document all that, though I don't know how specific she can get. I haven't talked to her in a few days. I can get what she has to you, if you want it."

The long silence on the other end was murderous. I could feel Chango seething.

"No need. If Ursula says it's so, then it's so. Did this screw up anything you're doing?"

"Not a bit, and we should leave it at that."

"Okay. Leave Burnside to me. Got it?"

"Absolutely."

The way I heard it later, Chango paid Burnside a visit. A short time later, Burnside announced that he was taking early retirement. The reasons were health-related. I'm sure they were.

As to what happened to Burnside after that, I never bothered to find out. I didn't care.

We never did find out who was trying to break our digital security. Ursula reported that it stopped at the same time I was, um, out of town. They never were successful and learned only what we wanted them to learn.

Ursula still wanted to hunt them down, and she was disappointed when I called it off.

Heenan called two weeks later. By then, life was pretty much back to normal, whatever normal is.

"How are you doin', buddy?"

"Okay."

"For real?"

"For real."

"Now that you've got some perspective, was it worth it?"

"Hell, I don't know. How can you tell?"

"You can't. Just don't beat yourself up," he said. "It had to be. Doing nothing would have been worse."

"Yeah, I know."

A LOOK AT: BORN FOR THE STORM

BY ROBERT WISEHART

He was destined to defy the odds long before Texas ever knew his name.

One of the most controversial and contradictory figures in American history, Sam Houston was a hero of two wars, badly wounded in both, famous for his marathon speeches, and known as a prodigious drinker, brawler, and carouser. A runaway teenager adopted by a Cherokee chief, he found a father figure in the tribe—while his other mentor, Andrew Jackson, would guide him for more than thirty years.

From his rough frontier upbringing and years among the Cherokee to his muddle-headed bravery at the Battle of Horseshoe Bend, Houston's early life was a grand adventure shaped by conflict and contradiction.

In a raw young Washington, Houston had his first taste of national politics and made his mark as an adroit politician. Elected governor of Tennessee, he faced a brief and tumultuous term before scandal forced him out of office—just as he would be forced out again years later. Even after a stunning fall from grace and a brutal street brawl with an Ohio congressman, Houston found a way to recover, never content to stay down for long.

AVAILABLE NOW

ABOUT THE AUTHOR

Robert Wisehart was born in Indianapolis, Indiana, and now is fortunate enough to live in Santa Fe, New Mexico.

In between Indianapolis and Santa Fe, he worked for many years as an award-winning reporter and columnist for newspapers in Florida, North Carolina, Louisiana and Northern and Southern California, plus occasional flirtations with radio and television as an on-air commentator. Such is the changing world that three of the four newspapers no longer exist.

Later, as a freelance writer, Wisehart did everything from write speeches to ghost books. He labored as a restaurant critic and for a brief time as a one of the dreaded horde of government consultants, two words that can mean almost anything but usually add up to not much. His work has appeared in more than 200 newspapers and 30 magazines, plus several digital outlets.

Wisehart and his wife, Dana, have been married for a lifetime and intend to make it a very long lifetime indeed. They have moved much, traveled well and Dana easily is the best thing that ever happened to him. Their two sons, Marc and Carl, live in New York City.

www.ingramcontent.com/pod-product-compliance
Lightning Source LLC
Chambersburg PA
CBHW030121260626
47156CB00008B/2744